FINDING FRIDAY

QUELL T. FOX

FLUFFY FOX PUBLISHING

Content Warning

Finding Friday is a reverse harem (MMFMM), full-length novel. This means the female main character will have more than one lover at the same time, which will continue throughout the book/series.

There are themes and situations in this book that may not be suitable for all, but especially not for readers under the age of eighteen.

These themes include descriptive sexual encounters and foul language.

CONTENT WARNINGS

This is a full list of trigger warnings for this entire series, not necessarily this book in particular.

- Mention of cheating (not main characters)

- Blood play

- Murder

- Murder of a child (flashback; not in detail)

- Mental health: schizophrenia, bipolar, PTSD

- Child abuse/neglect/inference of child sexual abuse

- Sexual assault

READING ORDER

ArcaNe BloodLines

This series is part of the Arcane Bloodlines Universe. The series are best read in this order:

Fighting Fate

Whispers of the Hidden Wolf

Set Me Free

The Awakening

You can view the rest of the books in the Arcane Bloodlines Universe too!

Arcane Bloodlines Universe

CHAPTER ONE

FRIDAY

Walking down the highway in heels is no easy task. As my feet ache and calves burn, I wonder why I decided to wear these hooker heels anyway. Oh, that's right. My boyfriend—excuse me, *ex-boyfriend*—is a cheating, lying asshole. Okay, so maybe that's not the *exact* reason why I put the heels on, but it was part of it. These heels paired with these jeans make my ass look delicious, and he needed to get one last glimpse of what he'd be missing out on for the rest of forever. Petty as it may be, it needed to be done.

That's what I keep telling myself, anyway.

So, why am I walking down this deserted highway, though? Well, as if my day couldn't get any worse, since you know, finding out my boyfriend has been cheating on me for who knows how long isn't bad enough, my car decided to fuck me over too.

Just died, right there on the busy highway—thankfully it rolled long enough for me to pull onto the shoulder and out of harm's way. It's also possible it ran out of gas. I'm not entirely sure at the moment, but I plan to get it all taken care of as soon as I find help.

My cell phone? It's broken. Maybe it was my fault, maybe it wasn't. Okay, it was! My anger got the best of me when I found him in bed with that bimbo, and *maybe* I whipped it at his head at some point. *Oops.* Can you blame me?

Life is looking pretty good right now, as you can see. No car, no phone, no home. Probably no money, either. That all depends on how quickly I can get to an ATM to take cash out before that shithead drains it on me.

I've been walking for a while now. Too long. I can't be sure exactly how long because I'm not one of those weirdos who can tell time by looking at how high the sun is and where Mars is positioned... or whatever. Not only that, but this heat is killer! I'm desperate for water. My mouth feels like it's been invaded by a desert.

On top of all that, I have no idea where I am, only that I am around ten hours away from where I lived. I *was* trying to follow a map, but who uses those things anymore? There was a sign back... I don't know, back *there*, that promised an exit with amenities in a few miles.

The few miles turn into what feels like a hundred by the time I make it to the exit without one car driving by. Not. One. Damn. Car. Leave it to me to find the one and only highway on the planet that people don't use. I mentally slap myself for not keeping my anger in check because I'd still have a phone right now if I had. Hopefully this town has a cell phone store. Based on my surroundings, I'm not sure a cell phone would work to begin with. I haven't seen a thing for miles other than fields, trees, and roads.

I drop my head back on my shoulders and let out a relieved breath when I finally reach the offramp, thrilled that I can make out the tops of buildings. I move quicker, pushing my legs to keep going. Just a little longer!

Of course, the one and only car I finally do see almost hits me on the curve of the off-ramp, and then has the audacity to honk at me. At me! Like, fucking *excuse me,* I'm walking here.

Finally, as I round the bend, a few small buildings pop into my line of view. Hopefully one of them will allow me to use the bathroom because I *really* have to pee. Which is weird considering my body feels like a dried-up vegetable.

Welcome to the town of Ellbrooke! the big green sign reads as I continue down the off-ramp.

Never heard of it.

I really wish I knew where I was. Am I even still in Indiana? Or did I cross a border somewhere? I'll figure it out later. Right now, I need a toilet and some water. Just not the water *from* the toilet.

The sign at the crossroads promises food, gas, restrooms, and more. *Thank fuck.* If I had to walk for another hour—shit, another five minutes—I can guarantee at least one, if not both, of my feet would fall off. Next time I find a boyfriend cheating on me, I'll be sure to use the heels to stab his eyes out and put sneakers on my feet.

I keep to the right, noting the sign told me there is a gas station, ATM, and a motel this way. Everything I need, all in one spot. The gas station is the first place I come to. Across the road is a sketchy-as-fuck looking motel. Perfect. That is, as long as I can get enough money out of the bank to pay for a room. If not, I'll be sleeping on the sidewalk. When I reach the storefront, noting the lot is free of cars, my feet are numb. Literally, numb. But still attached, so that's good. The bathroom is at the end of the building, a large sign telling me to ask an associate for the key. *Great.*

A chime sounds as I scurry into the small, compact store. The clerk behind the counter is a young kid with red hair, lots of freckles, and wire glasses—not even the cool kind. And they're crooked. He looks up from his handheld gaming system, but quickly looks back down. I walk directly to the counter, certain I'm going to pee my pants if I don't get a toilet stat. I swear I'm about to burst. I lean onto the counter, popping my chest out just a bit. If this kid tells me I have to buy something, I'm going to lose it. I can't wait that long, so I'm using what the good man gave me.

Flipping my mirrored sunglasses to the top of my head, I put on the best smile I own. Also the fakest, but guys can never tell the difference. They just see a pretty girl smiling at them and they're goo.

"Hi!" I chirp.

"H-hello, can I help you?" His voice squeaks. He tries to hide it by clearing his throat but fails miserably. There's no coming back from that one. Poor little guy.

"Yes, handsome." Not really... but you know, I gotta pee! "I really need to use the toilet, do you mind?" Sweeping my hair over my shoulder, I twirl it around my fingers, keeping the smile plastered to my face.

Come on, buddy. Just say yes. Hand over the key so I can empty my bladder.

He swallows hard, his Adam's apple bobbing up and down as he does. His eyes dart to my cleavage and he gives one slow nod, quickly bringing his eyes back up to meet mine. He hands me the long wooden stick thing that he pulls out from under the counter; attached to it with a zip tie is a tarnished gold key.

"Thanks, love." I wink before turning around. I then make a mad dash to the bathroom, my heels click-clacking on the cement all the way there. I'm convinced I am not going to make it. Which would be horrific. How would I explain that? And what would I change into? I have nothing with me. Everything is in my car! The only thing I took with me was my purse.

The bathroom is cleaner than I expected it to be. Under normal circumstances, homeless people wouldn't dare sleep in one to hide from a snowstorm. Trust me, I know, as I've been in many. But this? This is like a first-class station bathroom. I go in, do my business, wash my hands, and head back into the store as quickly as I can, the relief welcoming. Though, now that I'm not worried about peeing my pants, I realize how damn hot it is. I'm on the verge of turning into ash and getting blown away by the breeze.

The freckled kid is no longer standing behind the counter when I walk back in. I leave the key there anyway, assuming he couldn't have gone far since he's working and all. The blinking neon sign toward the back of the store catches my attention, telling me there is an ATM there. I pull my glittery black wallet from my purse, take out my debit card, and pray like hell there is money in the account. The machine takes my card, I enter my pin, and bounce from foot to foot in anticipation.

Click-clack. Click-clack.

"Yes!" I shout louder than I should have, unable to contain my excitement when I see the balance. Not a dime has been touched. Not yet anyway. Knowing I can only take a thousand from my account using the ATM, that's what I do. Bank rules suck. Maybe tomorrow luck will still be on my side, and I can take out another thousand or find a bank branch before the asshole does. I'll empty it at that point. It's the least he deserves after what I caught him doing.

I grab a few snacks and as many bottles of water as I can carry before heading up to the counter. They're cool on my skin and the feeling is welcomed. Redhead is back at the counter when I reach it. He scans my items and says, "That's going to be $23.82." It should be illegal to charge double for an item just because of convenience. I groan as I hand him my debit card, knowing I should get as much use out of it as I can and save the cash for emergencies.

"Do you know if there is an Americo Bank around here?" I ask as I take the plastic bag full of my stuff.

"Uh, not that I know of. Maybe a few towns over." He points a finger in the direction I just came from.

Wonderful.

"What about a tow place? Mechanic? My car is dead on the highway, may be out of gas, but I can never tell. The gauge hasn't worked in years." I do the hair flip thing again.

He perks up, a smile sliding across his thin, chapped lips.

"I can do it for ya. We got a tow truck here. Buck is on vacation, but he's showed me how to use it a few times, so I think it will be alright. Where do you need it to go?"

This kid is way too excited about this. Maybe not the best idea to let someone unskilled handle my car, but desperate times... you know how it goes.

"I'm hoping to head over to the motel across the road for a couple of nights." I peek out the window toward the motel looking for a sign that says there are vacancies. According to the big red letters, there are. "Looks to be my lucky day; they have vacancies. It's at least five miles back that way. A dark green Toyota." I hook a thumb behind my back because I couldn't tell you which direction that was if my life depended on it. And I don't have the slightest idea if five miles is accurate. Could be one, could be fifty.

"Oh, all right. I'd be happy to help. How about you give me your phone number, and I'll call you when it's all set?" He's digging around behind the counter, no doubt looking for paper and a pen.

Smooth little guy, isn't he?

"Wish I could, cutie, but my phone is broken. How about you just bring my car to the motel, and ask for my name? I'm sure they'll direct you to my room. Doesn't look like it's a busy place. Sound good?" I tap the counter with my manicured nail, smiling sweetly.

"That'll be just fine. What's your name?" He gives up looking for whatever he was looking for, and instead places his palms on the scratched counter, staring at me like I'm a lost cat who may run away if he moves too quickly.

"Friday McKay. See you soon." I flip my shades back down and click-clack out the door, purse in one hand and plastic bag full of goodies in the other.

Don't worry, babies, we're almost there, I tell my feet.

I start my trek across the road toward the motel that could be my new home for a while. I could sleep for a week, I think. Though, depending on the price of this place, a night or two may be my limit.

I'll be damned if I let all this negative bullshit bring me down, though. It's going to take more than a cheating douche to ruin my life. It's just a bump in the road, and I'll get over it. Just like I always do—like I always have.

The door to the motel office is being held open by a string that's attached to the wall behind it. How fancy. A very round, red-faced man sits behind the desk, his thin comb-over is blowing about from the small fan that's planted on the desk in front of him. His ugly brown eyes light up when I enter, but he doesn't stand.

"Well, hello there. What can I do for you, little lady?" He smiles, and I wish he hadn't. The few teeth left in his mouth are brown and rotted, and I swear I can smell the gingivitis from here.

Gag.

"Hi, sir. I need a room, please." I really try to keep my girly façade going, but it's never easy with a guy like this. I hate to be all judgy, but I can't help it. Sometimes, I'm a shallow bitch. Not just with guys though. It's people in general. I just can't stand most of the human race.

"Sure thing, my darlin'. For how long?" He spins in his swivel chair to fully face me.

"Definitely tonight, perhaps tomorrow too. See, my car just died and I'm on my way to visit my grandmother for her one-hundredth birthday. Can you believe it? One hundred. Anyway, I only need to stay as long as it takes for me to get my car fixed." I really hate lying, but what's a little lie when I'm in need? Desperate times... . Besides, my grandmother died a long time ago of an overdose, never even met her. I doubt she'd care that I'm using her for pity.

"Oh, I'm sorry to hear of your troubles. We have a few rooms open. Are you looking for anything particular?" He scans through a notebook, his finger dragging down the wrinkled page. Don't people use computers for this kind of thing?

"Whatever is cheapest. I'm running low on funds and trying to make sure I have enough to fix my car. And to buy Grams a present." I smile sweetly, my leg bouncing as I wait to see if he falls for it.

"Here's what I'll do for you because you caught me on a good day. Our normal rate is fifty-nine dollars a night, but I'll give you two nights for the price of one. How does that sound?" He winks and it literally kills me to keep the smile on my face. If he gets the wrong idea and thinks he's getting some sort of tip for this, in the physical manner, he's going to be the one getting a heel to the eye.

"Wow, that sounds amazing! You are a huge help, sir. Thank you so much." Clapping my hands together and doing a little bounce, I push back the vomit that crawls up my throat. It really does sicken me when I have to act like this. Why do guys fall for this shit? Yep, I'm swearing off guys. As of right now, I'm done with them. They're good for nothing, and nothing but trouble. I'm all set.

I hand the man my card, but he waves his hand at me. "Sorry, darlin', we only take cash." Of course.

"Oh... okay."

I pull three twenties from the giant wad I have in my wallet, and I do it with quick movements, not wanting him to know I'm playing him. He takes the cash, hands me back my change and a key. *A key.* Who still uses keys? I look around the small room and wonder if I've stepped into a time warp. Perhaps another dimension.

As I scan the office, I take in the white walls and floors which are in need of a cleaning. There is an empty water dispenser in the corner beside a yellow chair that's seen better days. I hope to hell the rooms are cleaner than the reception area.

The gruff voice pulls my attention back to the man.

"Room seven. Go out this here door and turn left. It's the last room on the bottom floor. Please, let me know if there is *anything*"—his emphasis on the word totally skeeves me out—"that I can do for you while you are here. Do you have someone taking care of your car for you?" His tone goes up a pitch or two, as if he's truly worried. I think he's just looking for more of a reason to ask for a favor that would involve me on my knees.

"I sure do. The young boy at the gas station across the road has offered to help me." I take a few steps back, letting him know I'm done with this conversation and ready to go.

"Todd?" he asks incredulously. "He doesn't know nothing 'bout cars. You sure you want him helping?" He shakes his head, disbelief written all over his face.

"I'll let him take a shot at it. No one learns anything if they don't get a chance to try." The saying was something I remember from high school. One of my teachers, Mr. Houghlin, had all kinds of cheesy quotes on poster boards plastered throughout his classroom. But for some reason, that one always stuck with me. I've never had a chance to quote it until now. It's possible the only reason I remember it at all is because he was the hottest teacher in school. Who doesn't love a hot teacher?

Before he says anything, I turn and leave, not wanting to know his opinion on the matter. I put a little pep in my step, knowing the creep is staring at my ass. I can't blame him; it really does look good in these jeans. It's a gift, really. So is the ability to use it confidently. It makes me kind of an asshole, I get that, but I'm okay with it. I flirt to get what I need, it's no big deal, really. Guys do the same. Why should it be okay for them to do it, but not us girls? It's not, and that is my point. Besides, I'm not hurting anyone, and it's become necessary to my survival. Something I learned at a young age. It's why I'm so good at it. Practice makes perfect.

I make it to the room quickly, wanting nothing more than to relax and take off these damn heels. The key slides into the lock with no problem, but I have to jiggle it to get it to turn. The room isn't nice by any means, but it will do. As long as there aren't any roaches, then it's fine by me. I've slept in enough motel rooms to know the signs of a bug infestation.

After I give it a once over, I decide I can relax. This one is clean... of bugs anyway. The rest of it isn't too bad either. I'd expected it to be worse. It's just your standard shitty motel room. Bed with scratchy sheets, nightstand, dresser with a TV on top, and a random chair placed in the corner. And the generic landscapes encased in gaudy gold frames for decor. Yep, typical motel room.

There is a robe hanging in the bathroom that looks clean enough to be safe to use. I really don't want to put my dirty clothes back on after all that walking in the heat, and I'd rather not leave the room in a towel. Even if it'll only be to my car and back. Unless Todd gets here sometime soon, I can grab my stuff from the car before I wash up. I didn't ask when he would be getting my car, and I should have. I wasn't thinking clearly. It's getting dark now, and I'm not sure what time anything closes or even when he'll be off shift.

The bathroom is not clean enough for me to want to spend a long amount of time in, so I take a quick shower and put on the robe. It smells like cheap detergent and the material is stiff and not at all comfortable.

I put my clothes in the sink to soak in warm water and the provided soap. I let them soak for only about ten minutes before scrubbing them, rinsing, wringing, and then hanging them over the shower rod to hopefully dry completely. I ignore the stains on the sink as I do this, telling myself they're just stains and not someone's bodily fluids.

I may seem like a snob, or like I come from money, but I'm not and I don't. The complete opposite, actually. I came from nothing. Absolutely nothing. That is why I am the way I am. I know what I came from, and how far I've come. I know I'm not better than anyone else, but I'm confident in who I am because of what I've overcome. I didn't lie on the floor when shit was bad. I faced it head on. Always have, and I'm not going to change now. I have done better for myself than a lot of people I know, and I'm very proud of that.

While I'm lying on the bed enjoying the bag of cookies I bought from the gas station, there's a soft knock on the door. I push my bag of chocolate chips to the side by the three empty bottles of water I've already sucked down.

Bright lights blind me through the peephole as I look through. As quickly as they are there, they're gone. Nope, there again. Gone. I pull back for a second, blinking the spots away from my vision. Assuming it's Todd because those blinding lights can only belong to a tow truck, I open the door.

"Hiya, Friday, I-I got your car over here. I can't do much in the dark, b-but if you'd like, I can come back in the morning to check it out for you." He juts his hand forward, dangling the car keys a little too close to my chest. I take them while taking a step back. The lights from the truck are so bright, I'm forced to squint and cover my eyes. That should be illegal.

"Oh, that would be so kind of you. You sure you don't mind?" His eyes wander down my body and slowly make their way back up to meet my eyes. I cock my head to the side, moving my still wet hair to one shoulder. The hair trick is gold. I wish I knew why, because really, it's kind of stupid.

"N-no, I don't m-mind." He shakes his head as he takes a step back. "I'll be back first thing in the m-morning."

"All right, you have a good night. See you soon." I wave him off.

"G-goodnight." He waves awkwardly before heading toward the large tow truck. I notice him stumble as I close the door. Poor kid is never going to get laid with that kind of awkwardness. If I weren't in such a shitty mood, I'd do it. I'd be doing the kid a favor. I'm in no mood for that though. I have no energy to help someone, let alone a pity-fuck.

I wait a few moments before looking through the peephole again. The flashing lights are gone and nowhere to be seen, even in the distance. It's dark out there, other than the small light above my door. This small town even lacks streetlights, and the gas station Todd works at mustn't be 24-hours because it's pitch black.

Now that the coast is clear, I pull the door open and walk toward my car. He left it in the spot in front of my door, which is so convenient. The cool stone is soothing on my sore, bare feet. I make it to the car without stepping on something sharp, and I open the trunk then reach for one of the giant black trash bags. In a hurry, I shoved all of my things into bags, then tossed them in the trunk. I drop the heavy bag to the ground, and it lands with a loud plop. The second one is just as heavy, and I barely get it out. How did I get these things in here?

"You hiding a dead body in there?" The deep voice comes from above. Instinctively, I look up to see what kind of nosey bastard is up there watching me like a creep. There's a man on the second-floor landing, his forearms leaning on the metal railing that's seen better days. It's hard to make out his features in the dark, but I can see his hair is perfectly in place, and the outline of muscles popping out of his tight shirt. He's nothing more than a silhouette standing against the dim light of the hotel door lamps. He steps back from the rail as he flicks his cigarette away. My eyes follow it as it lands a few spots down, sending sparks flying as it does. Bastard hasn't heard of an ashtray? My gaze slowly goes back to him.

"Wouldn't you like to know?" I retort. He breathes out this rumbling, husky laugh as he walks away, shaking his head. He disappears from my view, and a moment later, I hear the click of a door as it shuts.

I close the trunk and drag the bags into the room, hoping the entire way they don't tear at the bottom. There has to be *something* in these bags to wear. I made sure to grab as much of my stuff as possible since I don't plan on going back there. *Ever.* I also didn't want the douche to have the opportunity to be an even bigger douche and throw my stuff away. That is something he would do. He's *that* level of petty. Way worse than me. I lock the door behind me, leaving the bags by the door and plop down on the bed, sending the water bottles flying onto the floor. Oops. The stress of the day is finally taking over. I can barely keep my eyes open. I promised myself I wouldn't let this situation bring me down. Yeah, I loved him... still love him? I don't know. But obviously, he doesn't love me. I'm upset and hurt, but he doesn't care, so neither will I.

That's all there is to it.

Chapter Two

CALLAN

Our first stop is in a tiny town named Ellbrooke, population 6,317. The guys would never believe me, but I have heard of it before. Well, it's possible they would believe me because they know better than to doubt me when I state a fact.

"Did you guys know this town was once well-known for its Jam Festival?" The only one who pays me any mind is Lenny. He only gives me a quick glance, but it's something. "It only started to lose its notoriety twenty-two years ago when the mayor died, and they elected a new one. This one, Franklin Dodgson, tried to continue the same traditions, but he fell short. The townspeople slowly started to care less and less about the Festival and other town traditions." Blank stares meet me, and I'm not surprised. I tend to ramble about things most people find boring.

"Good info, buddy." Lenny's tone is sarcastic, but at least he was listening.

I'm shocked to see this motel is still up and running. I doubt they have tourists anymore. It's probably fueled by teenagers and cheating husbands. Even more of a reason why I don't want to be here, but alas, here I am.

I head to the bathroom for a much-needed shower. I'm sweaty after being in the car for hours, and when I'm sweaty, I'm uncomfortable. Being uncomfortable is not something I can tolerate. I get irritable and my skin crawls. Showering soothes me and as I wash away the sweat, I wash away the anxiety.

Of course the guys make fun of me for showering so much. They also like to poke fun at me for bringing the most clothes, telling me I'm worse than a woman, but because I shower so often, I need more clothes than they do. I couldn't possibly put used clothes back on. It doesn't really bother me, them picking on me. They do it out of a sort of brotherly love. It's been this way since we were kids. I wouldn't expect anything less from them at this point in life. We all have our parts, and this is mine.

As I scope out the bathroom, I almost change my mind. The ring stains on the tub have me weighing my options, but ultimately decide I need to wash up. The mildew and spots of mold in the corners won't jump off and attack me. This is one of the worst places we've stayed in during these trips. You'd be surprised how many motels in these small towns are nice. This one, however, is not.

At least the water stays hot for a while. The heat and refreshing steam tempt me to stay in longer, but the filth of the shower is starting to concern me. Plus, I can't be sure the other guys don't want to shower. They'd certainly let me know, most likely by barging in, but I can't be sure how long the hot water will last with the limited information I have. I'd feel bad if they had to take a cold shower. I wash my hair quickly, using my own shampoo. I'd die before using the cheap products these motels offer. I take the fresh bar of soap from the bag I packed it in and use it to wash my body, pausing when my fingertips graze over the large scar on the side of my belly button. A day I will never forget, though I certainly wish I could. I push the horrible memory from my head and finish up.

I put *two* towels on the floor before stepping out of the shower. I don't want my bare skin to touch the floor... ever. After I'm done drying, I step into the slippers I left by the door before grabbing another lazily folded towel off the shelf above the toilet. Looking down at it, I am suddenly appreciative of the fact I don't have to sit while I pee. I towel dry my hair and then wrap the towel around my waist. I run my fingers through my hair, making sure it will dry in the proper place. If it were morning, I'd blow dry it, but once I go to sleep, it'll get messed up and I've wasted my time.

I don't like wasting my time.

I'll tend to it in the morning.

I drop the towel to the floor and pull on my sweatpants. Stepping out of the bathroom, I find Lenny and Alec each taking up a bed, so I guess it's my turn to sleep on the floor. I huff out a sigh. I hate sleeping on the floor, but Maddox and Lenny will share a bed, neither of them cares about stuff like that. I don't think Lenny knows what personal space is. But there is no way Alec would share a bed with anyone, and three of us can't fit in one of these beds. Normally, the odd one would crash on the couch. This room doesn't have one.

Chapter Three

Maddox

I open the door to the tiny motel room that all four of us are sharing and step inside. As annoying as it is squishing into one room with these guys year after year, I look forward to it. Though I'll never admit it out loud. I'm not a feelings type of guy, and I don't plan to start now.

The door shuts behind me, and I can't get that girl out of my head. There is something about her. She's one of us, I know it. I can feel it in my bones. I felt it as soon as she got here. I knew someone like us was nearby. It's my job as the self-appointed head of our little group to watch out for anyone who could be a potential threat, and normally, the only others who are a threat to us are those like us. Humans are too ignorant to know the difference. It's quite embarrassing, honestly. They could see something magical happen right in front of their face, and because they can't logically explain it, they'll just deny it happening at all. Fucking humans.

I won't tell the guys about her yet. I don't think they'll take it well. We've been on these trips too many times, for too many years. Never with any luck. Normally people find their mates easily, they are naturally called to one another, pulled close together, but for us? Nothing has been easy. Not since we were children. So why would it be any different now? We go on this "vacation" every year—if that's what you want to call it—in search of our missing mate. The one to complete us. It's something we decided to do when we realized she wouldn't be coming to us. Ideally each person feels a calling toward one another, no matter where they are in the world and, eventually, they all find each other. It's not an obvious thing. You don't wake up and have a feeling your mate is across the country, but something will pull you closer together until you find one another. For us, though? It's crickets. And it doesn't make a lick of sense. After years of us being together and no one showing up, we knew we had to do something.

Each year, we drive to nowhere in particular, hoping one of us will get a pull to one place or another. It's never happened. I didn't get a feeling to come here either, I just did. Then, there she was. Because she *is* our she. I at least know that much.

The feeling isn't strong, not like it was with the guys, but it's there, faint and sweet, and the more I think about it, the more it feels right. But she came here *after* us. We've been here for a few hours now and not a single other person was checked in when we got here. I know because I asked the guy at the desk when I paid for our room. I always ask, wanting to know what kind of place we're walking into. Was *she* pulled here? She seems oblivious to what I am to her. That, or she's really good at pretending. Neither of those make sense. Why wouldn't she feel it? If she had, I certainly would have noticed the recognition in those golden eyes of hers. I've been waiting years to see it in someone. And if it's the latter, if she's pretending not to feel it, why? Why ignore a mate?

I stood on the balcony, smoking my cigarette, and I watched her emerge from beneath the balcony. My eyes went to her immediately, like a hawk homing in on its dinner. At first, I thought there was something wrong with her. She was walking funny, like she had been hurt, and the concern I felt was the first sign something was up. Then I realized she wasn't hurt at all; she was just stupid. Who the hell walks around in a town like this with no shoes on? Who knows what is on the ground. Is she trying to catch something?

I knew the moment she was close, though I'll admit at the beginning I didn't know the source of the feeling, just knew I felt different. A sense of relief washed over me, like maybe this was it. I'd been paying extra attention to our surroundings for the last hour because of it. But then I saw her, and there was nothing on her end. Not a single thing. And the longer I sit here thinking about it, the more dread that burrows into my soul. Now, here I am, going back and forth with what the hell I should do about this.

These trips used to be fun and exciting. When we started this eight years ago, I may have actually considered it a vacation. It was a way for us to get away from our bullshit, from our past. A time to enjoy life and have fun. *Together*. Then, slowly over the years, it stopped being fun and turned into a chore. Now, none of us really enjoy it, and I'm surprised we all still show up. Each of us still holds on to a small bit of hope, I think. It's the only thing that makes sense. We all know that we're more likely to find our missing mate if we're together.

The prophet warned us it would be like this. She said it would not be easy to find her, but when we did, she would fix everything for us. The prophet said we'd be in bad shape—which we are. We barely see each other anymore, barely speak. Our mate is supposed to bring us back together, help us resolve our issues. Her words have never faded in my mind through the years, and I think that's what keeps me going the most. Not the words specifically, but the thought of us being the way we once were.

The guys hold onto doubt too well. None of them believe in this mate stuff the way I do. They've given up. Lost hope. Lenny is the only one who takes my side and has my back when it comes to this. He's the one who trusts me the most, but probably only because he feels some sort of obligation to do so. Callan doesn't believe in that kind of thing—prophecies. Funny for someone like him, who is too smart for his own good and knows just about everything, to not believe in a prophecy. His reasoning is there are too many factors, too many things that could make it change. He's right, but still... have a little faith. Yet, he's the one who took the mate thing the most seriously in the beginning. And Alec? That guy is the most negative person on this planet, not that I can blame him after the shit he's gone through. I'm pretty sure he just thinks the world is out to get him at this point and thinks we're destined to be broken for the rest of our lives. The prophecy means nothing to him, they're just words he ignores—like everything else in this world. I truthfully can't believe I got him to come this year. I was certain it wouldn't happen. Certain he wouldn't even answer the phone when I called.

I find I keep going for all the guys, for all of us. For the idea that we can be whole one day, that we can be fixed and have something real, something worth living life for. Because deep down I love them, and always have. I could give up and let us fall apart. If I did, no one else would try. None of them would plan this. It would just be forgotten. But after everything we have been through in our lives, both together and alone, I can't give up. I can't let it all go to waste. I won't let all the pain and suffering we endured all be for nothing. Especially for Lenny.

The muffled sound of the shower pulls me from my thoughts. A quick glance around tells me it's Callan who's in there. Though, even if I hadn't seen Lenny lounging on one bed and Alec on the other, I'd guess it was Callan in there. The guy is not one for traveling. He hates staying anywhere that isn't his own sanitized house, and he showers so much when we travel because of it.

I pretend to busy myself with looking through my bag, but really, I'm trying to figure out what to do. Do I tell them, or no? Should I talk to her first? I catch the guys out of the corner of my eye, and I swear I would give my life for them. As much as they annoy the fuck out of me, they're my brothers. My life. My god damn mates.

I have to tell them.

They deserve to know.

We need this.

Chapter Four

LENNY

Callan finally gets out of the bathroom. I swear he spends more time in there than any woman ever could. I figure now is as good a time as any to find out what the plan is *this time*. This is our first stop, and even though every year we do basically the same thing, maybe this year we'll do something different.

Oh, please, let this year be different.

"What's our plan, Mad?" He doesn't like the nickname; he doesn't like any nickname I give him. This one is my favorite, though, because it does just that... makes him *mad*. "How long are we staying here for?"

"I think I found her," he says nonchalantly, and to no one in particular. My eyes go from him to Callan, who looks just as taken aback and confused as I feel. Then there's Alec, who ignores anything being said... as usual. The world could be exploding around us, and he'd be oblivious to it.

"Who?" Callan asks, standing by the door to the bathroom with a perfectly shaped brow raised. He probably thinks he didn't spend enough time in there, and he's contemplating going back in for a few more minutes. He sure wasn't in there as long as he usually is.

"*Her,*" Maddox says with a little more effort this time.

"You mean her? Like *the* her?" I ask.

"Yeah, that's what I said, shitbag." His insults don't bother me, I find them funny. He comes up with some creative names sometimes. Callan, on the other hand, always gets offended. Even though he tries to act like he doesn't, he's awful at pretending. Thankfully, this one was directed toward me, and I don't have to deal with them fighting again. Listening to them fight is like being a child back at home all over again. It's possible I have PTSD over that shit, but who knows?

"How do you know?" Callan asks, running his fingers through his damp hair.

"I just know," Maddox snaps back in the middle of folding a shirt. The same shirt he's been folding since he came in from outside. I'm more observant than he gives me credit for. I guess I'm to blame for that though. I let him believe I'm dumber than I actually am.

"That's a load of shit, Maddox, and you know it. Are your spidey senses tingling or something? Jesus Christ," Alec explodes.

And here we go.

"Alec, calm down and let's listen to what he has to say," Callan urges.

When it comes to Alec and Maddox, Callan plays peacekeeper. The two of them butt heads like crazy. They're both too stubborn and pigheaded to get along now-a-days.

Alec doesn't fight much with Callan or I because we know how to deal with him. It's easy: just ignore him. But when it comes to Callan and Maddox, *I* have to be the peacekeeper. I, on the other hand, try not to fight with any of them. These guys are like my big brothers. We've been together since we were kids, they all kind of raised me, more specifically Maddox. If it weren't for them, I'd probably be dead.

"No, I'm done listening to him and his bullshit. I shouldn't have fucking come. I don't want to be here. This whole trip is a joke. We never get anywhere, and it's a waste of my time. I could be home right now, working. Fuck you guys." Alec scrambles off the bed and storms toward the door. If he could have slammed it, he would have, but these motel doors aren't made for slamming. Probably a good thing. It's possible he'd have taken the thing clean off if he had.

CHAPTER FIVE

ALEC

This shit with our missing mate is getting old. I knew I shouldn't have come this year. I almost didn't because I'm over it. I told myself this would be the last year I played along with their game, and trust me, it will be. It's a huge waste of time when I could be home working and making money, catching up on all the bills I have. The bills I inherited from my shitty parents and bitch of an ex. The guys have offered to help, but I don't need their help. I can do this myself, and I plan to. As soon as I stop wasting my time on useless fantasies.

I don't know what the hell is wrong with Maddox, making a comment like that, to what? Get the other guys excited for something that isn't going to happen? How can he say something like that when we've been here only a few hours, and we haven't spoken to anyone? Did he pull a girl out of his ass while he was outside having a smoke? I don't fucking think so.

Part of me wants to believe him, wants everything to be alright, to be the way it should be, but it won't because that is my fucking luck. My life has *always* been shit. Ever since I was born to an alcoholic, drug addict, murderous bitch of a mother, it's been shit and it hasn't ever been better since. Yeah, I have the guys, but what does that get me? We argue most of the time and can't stand to be around each other, even if it's only a few weeks out of the year. Outside of that, we're practically strangers. Lenny and Maddox spend the most time together since they live in the same city. Lenny is the only one who really tries to talk to me throughout the year. It's like he's desperate to keep us together—the only family he has left. Little does he know how fucked up family is, and it really doesn't mean a damn thing. Sometimes, I want to tell him he shouldn't try so hard. He'll only be disappointed in the end.

I swear Callan could go without seeing any of us for the rest of his life and wouldn't lose sleep over it. He's some hotshot professor at some fancy private school. Well, fucking good for him. He's happy with his life and doesn't need the trouble we give him, messing up his perfect daily routine. I don't know why he comes either. Clearly, he's doing just fine for himself. So, what's the point? Do they still have hope for this? For us? Pretty fucking sure no one in the history of our kind has waited this long to find their mate. She's probably dead, or never existed at all because that's how fucked the universe is when it comes to me.

It occurs to me after I've been walking for a while that I have no clue where I am. Not that it matters; these stupid small towns are impossible to get lost in. They're all the same. A gas station, a shitty motel, a Sheriff's office, who is also probably the mayor. Then you have a bunch of small, family-owned businesses that probably don't make enough money to survive, yet somehow stay open year-round. One elementary school, one middle school, one high school. All with perfect students, who grow up to be perfect adults, and live their perfect lives.

The bright white flash of lightning off in the distance catches my eye, and I decide it's time to turn back. If I get caught in the rain, I swear it will be my breaking point. The loud roll of thunder comes only a few seconds later, so I pick up the pace.

I should have fucking stayed home.

Chapter Six

FRIDAY

It's too early to be awake, that much I know. I roll over, squinting my eyes toward the clock to make out the time as I hear another knock on the door. 7:43 a.m. Yeah, definitely too early to be awake. I groan, rolling out of bed and dragging my feet to the door. Looking through the peephole, I see Todd standing outside with a huge grin on his face. Begrudgingly, I open the door.

"Good morning," he says too happily and too loudly. "Sorry, uh, d-did I wake you?" So, he's smart, good for him.

"You did, but it's okay." I put on a tired smile, blinking my eyes to clear the sleep.

"Sorry about that." He scratches the back of his neck and shifts on his feet "I just need the keys…"

"Right, yeah. The keys. One moment please." I hold a finger up and walk away from the door, letting it fall shut as I grab them off the dresser by the TV. I make it back before it closes completely, snatch the handle and tug it open. "See you soon, Todd." I hand him the keys and close the door before he starts talking more.

Too early for words. Need more sleep.

I crawl back into bed, throwing the blankets over my head, fully intending on getting more sleep, and it comes all too easily.

The next time I wake up, it's at a more reasonable hour. I don't want to get up, but I also don't want to go back to sleep. I lay in bed for a while, enjoying the silence and the comfort of the bed. There is something about motel beds that make sleeping easier. Or maybe it's just knowing I'm sleeping without a cheating, lying asshole? Could be both.

My stomach starts to growl. I should get a proper breakfast. I crawl out of bed and dig through the bags of clothes and pull out something comfy to wear—a pair of jean shorts and a plain white T-shirt. When I stand, I spot the heels haphazardly tossed in the corner and I contemplate throwing them in the garbage. After walking miles in them, I'd love to watch them burn—along with every other pair of heels I own. Going into the bathroom, I wash my face and rinse my mouth out with the complimentary mouthwash, since I don't have a toothbrush with me. I scoop my dark auburn hair up into a messy bun and slide on some flip-flops—that feel like Heaven on my feet, by the way—and call it a day.

I grab my purse and the room key—don't want to forget that. I head right to the main office. It's empty of people, but I find what I am looking for. Along the left wall there are loads of flyers left by local businesses and people coming and going through the motel. Places like this always have a spot designated for small businesses. On the corkboard above the table, I find a list of restaurants that are close by, the nearest one is only a half-mile—according to the sticky note that's attached to it. I look over the table and grab the pamphlet I need. On the front flap is a small map showing where it's located. I find the place on the map and backtrack to where the motel is. When I leave here, I need to turn left then go straight for three blocks and make another left turn. Simple enough.

If my feet could talk, they'd be squealing with excitement right about now. The same way my stomach would be, knowing I'm about to get some real food. Tucking the paper into my purse, I walk out the door. The parking lot is empty aside from one Jeep that's diagonal from where my car was parked. My eyes move up to the now-empty second floor where the nosey bastard was standing last night. A quick chill runs over my body as I think about him, trying to recall what he looked like. The nice hair, the muscles, that husky laugh... I ignore the emotions rushing through me and start walking to my destination. I swore off men yesterday. I just got out of a long and stressful relation-ship. The last thing I need is some bad boy crushing my heart further.

It's a nice day today, good for walking. The sun is shining; a cool breeze is blowing. It must have rained last night because the ground is damp and there are small puddles here and there. I'm thankful it isn't as hot as it was yesterday.

By the time I get to the restaurant, my stomach is cramping. Either from walking, or starving, or both. And my feet aren't as happy as I thought they'd be. Apparently, they are still mad at me about yesterday, and they are making it known. They're sore and throbbing. I glance around the lot I'm in, hoping to find a nail salon. A pedicure and foot massage would perk me up. But no such luck. The only thing I see from here is a hardware store and a fabric store. I forgot where I was for a minute—in the middle of nowhere.

The breakfast rush must be over as the lot is mostly empty. The sign just inside the door tells patrons to sit themselves, so I sit in the back corner, ignoring everything around me. I'm too hungry, and too physically tired to care. I'm soon greeted by a young girl with beautiful big blue eyes and tan skin. I'm kind of jealous. She leaves a menu on the table and says she will be right back with my coffee. I look over the menu as I wait, deciding on an omelet. No matter what I get, I know it will be good. Small diners always have fantastic food. My stomach is telling me I'm starving, but I don't have much of an appetite. The stress of yesterday is still taking a toll on me. I don't like to eat when I'm pissed off. I don't want to be angry; I just want all of this to be behind me, but I need time to get over it.

The waitress returns a few moments later and the delicious smell of coffee perks me right up. I give her my food order as I pour cream into my coffee. I take a sip of the almost too hot liquid, then lean back against the cushioned seat. I'm lost in thought when a bunch of loud voices pull me back to the present. I look up to see four really good-looking guys walk in. They're laughing and talking to each other, very loudly. Clearly no consideration for others. Unfortunately, it doesn't take away from their looks, but that's how it is, isn't it? Hot guys, no manners. I narrow my eyes at them as they take a seat in the corner furthest from me. As I watch them with curiosity, I realize one of the guys is the one from last night. The nosey asshole. I'm sure of it. That perfect hair is recognizable, along with those muscles. He looks up, catching my gaze, and I quickly look away, not wanting to poke the bear. Maybe if it were a real bear, yeah. I'd totally poke a real bear. They are soft and cuddly. The fact that they can tear your face off with one swipe of their paw makes them that much more badass.

I bring my attention out the window, watching cars drive by and sipping my coffee until my food arrives. Thankfully, it doesn't take long. The waitress places my food in front of me and I take my time with it. I force each bite, knowing I need to eat. I'd rather fill up on coffee, but that's not a good idea. The omelet is good, really good, but I can only finish half. I take so long to eat that the four guys are finished before me, and the balcony guy winks at me as he walks out the door.

I scoff. What an arrogant asshole.

The young waitress, named Kelsey, walks over and asks if I'd like a container for the unfinished half of my omelet. I decline because I don't want to carry it with me while I walk. She removes my plate and heads toward the kitchen, but she doubles back almost instantly. "By the way, those guys that just left, they paid for your food. So, you're good to go."

My nose scrunches up and a frown falls on my lips.

Why would they do that?

"Oh, okay. Thank you," I say.

"You have a great day now." She turns and disappears through the swinging doors.

"You too." My words come out quiet, a bit dazed. That really threw me off. I wasn't expecting my breakfast to be paid for, but I'll take what I can get. Even if it's from a weird guy who seems to have an eye for me.

Before leaving, I ask the waitress where I can get a new phone, and she directs me to a phone store a mile down the road, farther away from the motel. *Fantastic.* I thank her and leave, heading toward my next destination. My feet are complaining before I can even make it out the door.

As I'm walking, I regret not putting on my sneakers. Why don't I think about these things beforehand? I swear, sometimes I have horrible decision-making skills. Okay, most of the time. And, as if bad luck is attracted to my already negative state, the sky turns an eerily dark gray in a matter of minutes. Just my luck. I better make it to and from the phone store before it starts to rain. As luck would have it, it literally starts to downpour the minute I set foot in the store.

Just fucking great.

Not wanting to worry about it now, I walk toward the back of the store, past the rows of electronics, stopping when I see the young blonde man behind the desk. He's tall and has way too much gel in his hair. He does smell good though. Some kind of expensive cologne that I can't pinpoint.

"Good morning, welcome to Darney's Electronics. How can I help you today?" His voice is high-pitched and too happy. He's a salesman through and through. Before responding, I look at his name tag. People react to you better when you use their name. It shows you're paying attention or something, personalizing the conversation and all that jazz.

"Hi, *Brad*. Actually yes, you can help me." I pull the smashed phone from my purse, laying it on the counter in front of me. "I need a new phone, and hopefully, everything from my old one can be transferred to the new one." My boobs aren't hanging out today. I'm not in the mood to pretend, anyway. It's a say-it-how-it-is kinda day. No bullshit. Take it or leave it.

"Of course! I'd love to help you with that. What kind of phone are you interested in? Do you have insurance on this thing?" He picks it up and wiggles it between his fingers.

"Nope, no insurance, and whatever cheap phone you have that's similar to that thing." I point to the old phone, the one I've had for way too long. I guess this could be a good thing. New phone for my new life.

"There is a deal going on right now. The newest smartphone is half off... *if* you pay in cash."

New? Even at half the price, it's probably more than I can afford.

"How much would that be, Brad? I'm running on a budget here." I tap the counter with my nail.

"You caught me on a good day, so I'm gonna give you a break. If you buy the new phone, on top of the half off, I'll give you my discount."

"Numbers, Brad. Talk to me in numbers," I say, letting boredom creep into my tone.

"Three twenty-five, even."

"Hmm, that's a little above my—"

"Okay, here's what I'll do, final offer. I'll give it to you for two-fifty."

"You don't get a lot of business around here, do you?"

"No, not really," he admits, blowing out a breath and looking at me with a desperate gleam in his eye.

"I'll take it," I say as a smirk crosses my lips.

An hour later, I'm waiting out front of Darney's, hiding under the tiny awning that is doing absolutely nothing to shield me from the rain. The bus should have been here ten minutes ago, but I haven't seen one drive by at all since I've been at the store. I couldn't have missed it...

I decide to wait a few more minutes before giving in and walking in the rain. At this point, I really don't care if I get soaked. Just as I am about to start walking, the bus pulls up and I jog to the open door and up the steps. *Thank god.* Putting exact change into the dispenser, I take a seat toward the front. I pull out my brand-new, bright red phone and start going through it.

Twenty-four missed calls, four voicemails, thirty-two texts, and nine new emails. I don't want to deal with any of this right now, so I drop my phone back into my purse with a sigh. I know full well they're all from the douche. It's not like I have friends or anything. I haven't logged into any social media yet, but I'll bet he's messaged me on every account I have. He never was one to let things go. Me, on the other hand? It's so easy to cut the cord.

The bus driver lets me off in front of the motel reception area, even though it's not a regular stop. I'm the only person on the bus and I think he can tell I'm not from around here. I'm thankful he takes mercy on me since it's downpouring and all. I thank him a hundred times before leaving the bus. I've noticed people in this town are really friendly. More friendly than I'm used to. I start to worry I've happened upon one of those crazy towns where the people kidnap tourists to wear their skin or keep them locked in the basement as a pet. I hope not. God, I really hope not.

As I walk back to my room—using the second-floor landing as cover—I notice that guy leaning over the railing again, having another smoke. I walk closer to the building, hoping he can't see me. I get a strange feeling when he's near me, like my skin is tingling. I feel on edge, and not in a good way. It's creepy. He tried starting a conversation with me last night, and today, he paid for my food... I'm in no place to make friends, especially male friends. No thanks, buddy. Besides, I'm a sucker for guys with tattoos and muscles. I really need to keep my distance.

"I don't get a *thank you* for buying your breakfast?"

Dammit, I thought I was safe when I made it to my door without a word.

Fan-fucking-tastic. There goes my ignoring him. What is with this guy? I back up enough so I can see him but stay under enough, so I don't get soaked.

"That all depends. Why *did* you pay my bill? I am capable of paying for my own things, you know." I place my hand on my hip. His eyes shine with laughter as he takes me in.

"What? A guy can't buy a beautiful girl breakfast?" *The audacity.*

"Oh, please. Haven't heard that desperate line before. Sorry, dude, but I'm not interested."

With that, I walk into my room and lock the door behind me. I double check the latch is secured, just in case. You never know what kind of nutcases you'll run into on the road, especially in a small town like this. Norman Bates, anyone?

Stepping out of my flip-flops, I lay face down on the bed and unlock my new phone. Going through all of these notifications isn't what I want to do, but I should get it over with. As I suspected, most of the missed calls are from him. A few were from numbers I don't recognize. They were probably telemarketers wanting to tell me about the expiring warranty on my car. No way in hell that POS has a valid warranty. The thing is older than me! It's not the best car, but it's been reliable for years. I hate that this may be the end of it. I guess it's only fitting though. Rid myself of all the old junk holding me down, and start fresh...

I'm thankful my new phone has a voicemail to text option. His bullshit words that usually send my anger into overdrive are easier to tolerate when they're written across the screen. Of course, he's still a shithead, though. That will never change. Next, I go through the texts. They start off with him telling me it wasn't what it looked like. Then the guilt strikes, aimed directly at my heart. Then, he's apologizing. Finally, yep, you guessed it—anger, gaslighting, and deflecting. Shocking, I know.

I clear the notifications, contemplating blocking his number but decide against it. I'd rather know what's coming than be blindsided. If he stops texting and calling after a few days, I'll know he's over it. But if this goes on for weeks, I'll know to watch out for him escalating. He was never an overly angry person, not really. I saw him get mad for valid reasons, but he was never abusive. Not physically, anyway. He was jealous, sometimes extremely, and now I know why. Our relationship was mostly normal. It seemed like things were going well. Then again, they always seem that way, don't they? Four years of my life down the drain over some blonde bitch from his office that he met less than a year ago.

He could have at least broken up with me first. I think that's what bothers me the most. If he didn't want to be with me, he should have said it. I'd have been fine with it. I mean, it would have taken time, but if he didn't want to be with me, I wouldn't have begged. Problem is, he's a greedy bastard. He needed both of us. I gave him security, but she gave him excitement. Fucking dickhead.

With a huff, I get out of bed and head into the bathroom. Eyeing the tub, I mull over whether I want to do this or not. It isn't the worst tub I've bathed in, but it's sketchy. I really could use a bath right now. A good soaking in water so hot it'll feel like my skin is melting... yeah, that's too tempting to pass up. Letting out a sigh, I grab one of the half-folded towels from the shelf above the toilet, wet it, and start scrubbing the tub using the soap on the sink. Nothing comes off, and now that I know for sure it's just stained and not bad cleaning, I'll live.

I turn the knobs to fill the tub, and take the small bottle of bubble bath to dump in. It's the cheap stuff and smells okay at best, but it'll do. The lavender goop seeps out of the bottle slowly and mixes with the water, forming pitiful bubbles that wouldn't even make a child happy. Stripping my clothes off, I leave them on the bathroom floor and get into the tub. I allow the water to get as high as possible before I turn it off and lay my head back against the towel I rolled up.

Deep breaths, in and out. Steam and lavender fill my nostrils, relaxing me a little more as each second ticks by. I raise my fingers out of the water, watching the little droplets fall off quickly. I do this over and over, dipping my hand in and lifting it, watching the droplets fall. It's distracting enough to keep my mind clear, and it relaxes me further. After a while, I notice the temperature of the water is more cold than hot. Unsure of how much time has gone by, I switch the lever down to empty the water from the tub and stand.

I reach for the towel I left on the counter and wrap myself in it. I walk to the mirror and wipe away the condensation with my hand. My skin is paler than normal, dark circles are starting to form under my eyes. My honey-colored irises, normally bright and intense, now look dull and dreary. I've always liked my round face, thinking it makes me look younger than I am. Not that I'm old by any means but twenty-seven is only a few years short of thirty. And thirty is that scary age. The one where you feel obligated to have your life together, and if you don't, then you're a failure and completely suck at life.

I pick up a second towel to dry my hair. The dark, auburn strands fall down my face in damp waves. So, what if it isn't my natural hair color? No one needs to know that. It's always been my color of choice, ever since I was able to buy a box of hair dye with my own money. Mom would never buy something like that for me. Hell, she barely provided me with the things I needed to live.

Leaving the wet towels in the corner of the room, I dig out comfy clothes to wear, throwing them on before plopping onto the bed to watch TV. The realization hits me that tonight is the last night I have to stay here. I'm sure I could pay for another, but that's just delaying the inevitable.

Now that I have a working phone, I can go online and check the bank account instead of walking over to the ATM. It's only across the street, but I've done more walking in the last two days than I have done in a long time, and my body is sore. I should have stopped at the ATM before coming back here, but I spaced it out.

Checking the bank app, I realize that douche was kind enough to leave me five hundred dollars in the account. Everything else is gone.

How fucking sweet of him.

CHAPTER SEVEN

FRIDAY

My mind won't stop, and even though my feet are going to be mad, I need to move.

I slip on my flip-flops and head out the door to walk across the street to the gas station in search of Todd and my car. When I walk into the store, there is an older woman behind the counter. She looks like she may have a shotgun hidden beneath the counter, one she knows how to use all too well. I walk to the back of the store, hitting the ATM first, wanting to remove the last of the money before it's gone. I curse to myself when the balance shows up.

Zero.

It's literally zero.

God fucking dammit!

I only have myself to blame. I should have stopped by earlier. Annoyed with myself—and life in general—I go to the freezer section and grab a few frozen meals. Normally, I would never eat this type of thing; they are terrible for you, and they taste like cardboard, but they're cheap and I'm working on a budget right now. I don't have much of a choice.

The older woman takes the items and rings them up. I don't even get a greeting, just a grunt and a dirty look.

"Hi, ma'am, is Todd working today?" I ask as nicely as I can, handing her a twenty to cover the items.

She huffs before answering. "You trying to buy drugs?" She slaps my change onto the counter, and I startle at the loud sound.

"Uh, no?" I choke out. What kind of business is this?

She narrows her eyes at me, and I raise an eyebrow. I'm not backing down from this old hag. So much for everyone around here being friendly... or maybe she was offering? I don't know which is worse.

"He'll be in soon," she practically spits out.

"Okay, he's helping me out with my car. Is it possible to—"

"Oh, is that your car out back? The one with the blown gasket?" Her lips turn up into what I think is supposed to be a smile. Is she happy that I just got horrible news?

"I fucking hope not!" My baby is dead? I place my hand on the counter to steady myself. "Sorry, I didn't mean to say that out loud. What kind of car is back there?"

"Some kind of Toyota. Green, I think. Shame. Those usually run forever." She shrugs like this isn't a big deal. Like this isn't life altering. Like I'm not completely screwed now.

I mean, I already knew that, but hearing it? Knowing this is my reality? Ugh.

"Damn. Yeah, I think that's my car. Do you have Todd's phone number?" She eyes me warily. "Better yet, here is my phone number. Could you please give it to him when he gets in? Ask him to call me as soon as he can." I write my number down on an old receipt I find at the bottom of my purse and slide it across the table to her. She picks it up and pockets it. "Please, it's important." She blinks but says nothing. I grab my bag and go, figuring I could stand here all day and she won't say another word.

I'm just about to the door when my phone rings. I dig it out of my purse to check who is calling. *Private Caller.* No thanks. I click the side button twice to end the call and shove the phone back into my purse. As I dig my key from the dark depths of my purse, a chill runs up my spine, so cold, it makes me shiver. Someone is standing behind me. I just know it. I shift the key between my fingers, ready to stab a fucker in the eye. I'm not stupid enough to try and get into my room; that's how they get you! Instead, I spin around, preparing myself for a fight only to find the creep from upstairs leaning on one of the support beams. My god, was he there the whole time? Was I so in my own world I didn't even notice? The smirk on his face screams arrogance, along with the way he's standing. It's just... cocky. But my god, is he sexy as hell. The muscles, the tattoos, the dark hair and steel gray eyes. He's definitely the type that'll fuck you and then act like he doesn't know you. I need to stay far, far away.

"Can I help you?" I ask, folding my arms across my chest. The plastic bag with my frozen meals inside sways, the crunching of plastic echoing around us.

"Why are you here?" he asks simply. There is no emotion, no nothing.

"Excuse me?" I choke out. What the hell kind of question is that. Am I not allowed here?

"What are you doing here?" he asks me again, this time annunciating each word like I can't understand English. Cocky asshole.

"That is none of your damn business," I snap.

I should leave now. I should go into my room to get away from him, but I've watched too many shows on murders to do that. He'd get the perfect opportunity to walk right in after me, trapping me inside with him. Which, if he weren't a murderer, could be fun, but I can't chance that. He's a lot bigger than me, and I'd never be able to fight him off. He is tempting. I could use a good rebound, but no. Not doing it. His smirk widens and I realize I'm staring... and he caught me. Dammit. "Please, leave."

"As you wish, beautiful." He turns and leaves, as simple as that. I stand there for a few moments, mouth hanging open. Was it really that simple? I just tell him to leave, and he does? Huh...

Once I'm confident he's gone, I quickly make my way into the room, locking the door behind me. I put my bag of frozen food into the tiny freezer, hopeful it will keep it frozen enough to stay safe to eat. I hear the muffled sound of my phone ringing again, I pull it out and again it says, *Private Caller*. I take a second to think and it pops into my head. Damn, I need to answer this!

"Hello?" I answer in a rush, hoping I'm not wrong.

"Hi, Friday? I-it's Todd."

Thank god!

"Yes, hi! How are you?" I sit down on the edge of the bed, hoping the woman at the store was wrong and he has good news to give me.

"I'm good, but I have some bad news. Oh, but I also have some good news too."

"Bad news first." I roll my eyes and plop back onto the mattress, already knowing what he's going to say.

"The head gasket on your car is blown and fixing it will cost a lot of money. Good news is the guy at the station wants to buy it for parts. Bill said he'll give ya a c-couple hundred for it."

Fuck. Off.

I roll my lips between my teeth, pushing away the rush of emotion. I haven't cried once since my life fell to pieces and I won't do it now. This is fine. I'll be fine. I'll get through it, I always do.

Think, Friday. What are my options? I can't do anything with the car. I certainly don't have enough money to fix it. I mean, maybe I do but then I wouldn't have a penny left to my name. I have to sell it. I have to get rid of it, save my money, and keep on with my plan. It's the only way.

"All right, that sounds good." I force the words out because nothing about this sounds good. "Could you do me one last favor though? All of my belongings are in the trunk. Could you bring them over to the motel for me before tomorrow morning? It's my last night here."

"Sure thing, Friday. I'll do it as soon as I'm done with my shift tonight, and I'll let Bill know to write up the paperwork for you."

"Thanks, Todd, you're the best." With that, I end the call.

I let out a shaky breath. What am I supposed to do now? I have nowhere to go and no car. I may be back up to a thousand dollars once I get the money for the car. That's at least one positive thing. But how far is a grand going to get me? Why does my life suck so hard? All this crap in a matter of two days. *Two days.*

The plan when I left was to drive back to where I came from. I refuse to call it home because it was never my home. I know plenty of people there, though, someone would let me crash on their couch. I could go to my mom's, but that is an absolute last resort. Almost not even an option kind of last resort. I'd prefer sleeping on the streets than staying anywhere near her. Hell, even the thought of being in the same town as her has my blood boiling. But now? With no car? I have no idea what to do. Literally, no idea. I barely have family and no friends at all. All the friends I did have weren't mine and never liked me much anyway. They only hung around with me because of doucheface. Not that I care because I didn't like them anyway. They were rude and stuck up. I wonder how many of them he was sleeping with. The more I think back on my life over the last four years, the more I realize I have no clue what the hell I was thinking. The more I realize how fucking lonely I am. I see how deep I've buried myself, how much I allowed myself to isolate from everyone.

What have I done with my life? I used to be proud of where I was and how far I went. I've always told myself that, repeated in my head like a mantra. But now, as I look back, I wonder if I've been making it all up. Have I been blind to what's going on around me? I mean, look at me. My boyfriend cheats on me and I suddenly have nothing. Did I really put my entire life into that guy? What did I do to deserve such a shit life? I must have been a real asshole in a previous one.

It's like I've been on autopilot for the last four years. Same boring shit every day. It was at least a little better when I was working, but then I got laid off. I never found anything that was worth doing after that. Nothing seemed good enough, and we didn't need the extra money because asshole made enough for both of us, and he preferred me at home and away from people. Why was I okay with that? My goal was to start school again. I guess I started getting lazy and was enjoying being content for a change. Funny how you don't realize how bad things are until you take a step back and look in from the outside. I guess me finding him balls deep in another woman was a blessing in disguise. This has to be my chance at a new beginning, a chance to do more than just exist. A chance to enjoy life.

I'm going to make it happen. I have to. I've gotten through too much bullshit in my life to give up now. If I can deal with everything else I've gone through, then I can deal with this. It's only a minor setback. That's it. I've got this. I can do this.

My phone dings, I pick it up to check who is texting me. It's a number I don't recognize, but I open it up anyway.

UNKNOWN: Hey Friday, it's Todd. I wanted you to have my number in case you may need anything else. Text or call any time, promise it's okay ;)

This poor, goofy kid. He's too nice for his own good. Maybe in a town like this, it works. I didn't grow up in a place like this, so I guess I *really* don't know. I have no clue what it's like living in a small town where everyone knows everyone. I've only ever lived in big cities.

I respond back with a thank you, and he tells me all my stuff will be here late tonight after work. Like he didn't already say that. He's just being nice, I know, but I'm in a bad fucking mood now. I wish I had friends to party with. Getting drunk sounds so good right now. I wonder what that guy upstairs is doing. Are they all up there? All four of them? No, that's a bad idea. *Stop thinking about the hot guys, Friday. We've sworn them off, remember?* It's bad enough that one guy keeps popping up at random trying to get my attention. He is hot as fuck, and the sex would probably be so good, but it's a trap! They lure you in with their good looks and satisfying sex, and then when they have their claws in you, they ruin your life. Nope. I am done with men. *Done.*

I allow myself to be miserable for a few more minutes before I get up. I need to go through my stuff. If I don't have a car, there is no way I can take all of my things with me. I have to sort out what I need and don't need. I can't lug everything with me now.

In my fit of rage, I ransacked our house and threw a bunch of random things into the bag—wouldn't be surprised if I find a frying pan or toilet paper. All I could think about was grabbing my stuff and going. There was no time to think, I just had to act.

I'm probably going to have to pay for another night at this motel. I don't want to waste the money on it, but I feel like I don't have a choice. Time is against me at this point, and I need more of it. I leave everything I've dumped out in a pile and make my way to the office. There's a different person behind the desk today; a middle-aged woman, her blonde almost white hair is up in a tight bun on the top of her head. Her long, crooked nose turns up at me when she sees me walk in. I know this type. Hates all other women, especially younger, prettier ones. She probably thinks I'm a hooker. Just great.

"Hi, I'm staying in room seven. I'm supposed to leave in the morning, but is there any chance I could pay for another night?" My voice is low and tired. I don't play games with her. One: I'm too tired. Two: They wouldn't work anyway.

"Let me check." She takes a minute to look through the scheduling book. They're either stuck in another decade or they don't have the money to upgrade to a computer program. Come to think of it, I don't even see a computer. "Another night in that room will be one hundred and twenty-nine dollars."

"What? Why? The guy the other night said it was only fifty-nine!" I'm so done with life at this point. I want to crawl into a cave and hibernate for the rest of forever.

"The other night wasn't a *Friday* night. It's our busiest night. The room rates go up. Take it or leave it," she snarls.

Not wanting to spend that much of my money on a place to stay, I decide to take my chances on something else.

"Thanks, but I'm good," I sass, then turn on my heel and stomp back to my room like a child. Will anything ever go right for me?

My foot hits something as I reach my room. I look down and find a small paper bag with a note attached. I pick it up and pluck the note from the bag.

I don't need a thank you.

-Maddox

My god, even his name is uppity. He probably has a matching pretentious last name to go with it. Something like St. Claire or Van Buren. I scoff, but I can't help the smile that crosses my lips at his thoughtful little note. I forget my anger for a moment, but just a moment. I quickly wipe it from my face, worried he's watching me. I can't let him win. Not that easily, not over a bag of food. I take it inside, sit on the bed, and open it up. I pull out a cheeseburger and fries. It smells delicious and I waste no time eating it, trusting it isn't poisoned. I'm not too proud to let something so delicious go to waste. When I'm done eating, not feeling the slightest bit guilty for not giving him a thank you, I finish sorting through my belongings.

It doesn't take long, and I only decide to keep a few things. I'll have to purchase a backpack to carry what I'm keeping, but the rest... well, I'm hoping Todd can do me one last favor.

CHAPTER EIGHT

FRIDAY

The clock shows it's past one in the morning, but that can't possibly be true, can it? I've spent the evening browsing the internet and drifting in and out of sleep because there is nothing else to do. This is kind of like a nice vacation, if only I had a home to go back to when it was over. I stretch and kick off the blankets; I need some air. My feet reach the rough surface of the rug and I walk quickly to the door. I unlock it and tug it open, leaning in the door frame while I suck in some cool air. It's the perfect night for a walk, but I'm just not up for it. Would also be the perfect night to sit outside in my backyard, lounging on a comfy chair, if I had one. After a few moments, I decide I should get to sleep. It may be the last night for a while that I'll sleep in a bed.

When I turn to go back inside, I notice an envelope on the door. I sigh out a breath and grab it before going inside. If this is that Maddox guy... I open it up to find two hundred dollars and a note stating it's for the car. I feel like there should be more involved than just someone handing me cash, but I don't care enough to ask questions right now. The car isn't in my name, neither is the insurance. Fuckwad can deal with the repercussions.

I send Todd a quick text thanking him and asking for one last favor. I hope he will have a place to store my extra things until I am able to get them—whenever that may be. My phone dings, letting me know there is a text. I check it immediately, hoping Todd answered me back and has some good news to give me.

Nope.

Doucheface: Baby, please talk to me. I'm sorry, come home!

Ding!

Asswipe: I miss you xoxo

Ding!

Fuckbag: I promise I'll change.

Ding!

Fucking pathetic.

I type out a reply that has more swears in it than necessary—okay, maybe they are necessary. But just before I hit the send button, I delete everything. He isn't worth my time, my anger, or my words. He isn't worth the dirt on the bottom of my shoe. He can kiss my ass and deal with what he did.

My phone dings again and this time I almost don't check it, but I'm glad I do. This time it is someone I want to hear from.

Todd: I'd love to help! I can keep that stuff as long as you'd like. I live alone, no one to worry about touching your things. I'll keep them safe.

I better make sure to not leave any panties with him... he'd probably hang them off the mirror in his car as an air freshener.

I send a short thank you back and let him know I have to be out of here tomorrow by eleven in the morning. He promises he will be here before that to get everything from me. He has been very helpful, and for what? I haven't done a damn thing for him... In fact, all I've done is make fun of him in my head. That's probably why shitty things keep happening to me. Karma knows what's going on in my head, and she's giving me what I deserve. I need to stop being so mean to people just because I'm grouchy.

I almost want to tell him to be here at eleven, so I can get as much sleep as possible. I'm going to miss sleeping in a bed. Honestly, for a split second, I consider asking him if I can stay with him, but that's just way too weird for me. I can't rely on this teenager to help me; I need to do it myself.

Going back to Shitville, Indiana won't be the worst thing. Well, if I have to stay with my mom it might be. I'll deal with that when I get there. When I leave tomorrow morning, I'm going to a bus station and taking the next bus back to Hell. Simple enough.

I wake to the sound of my alarm and snooze it. When it goes off the second time, I jerk awake remembering I have a bus to catch. I checked the times before falling asleep last night, which was really late, or early, depending on how you want to look at it. The bus is leaving in a few hours and the bus station itself is an hour from here. I could wait and catch a later bus, that would allow me to sleep longer...

Bad idea, I know. With scratchy eyes and a foggy head, I hop in the shower and take my time, all the while thinking this could be the last shower I get in a while. I have no idea what'll happen when I get back to Indiana.

When I'm done, I throw on a pair of jean shorts, a tank top, and my sneakers, knowing I have a lot of walking to do today. The weather channel said it's going to be a hot one. I prop the door open in preparation of bringing my bags out and leaving them there for Todd. I curse under my breath when I remember I was supposed to get a backpack. Dammit, I guess I'll just have to use the plastic bags I got from the gas station.

The heat outside is already setting in and I groan as it starts to take over the room. I pick up the first bag full of stuff that I'm not taking and lug it toward the door. As I reach it, I catch a glimpse of the four guys loading up their Jeep. They must be leaving today too. I stop just inside the doorway to watch, because I'll admit, they're really nice to look at. I pull my large sunglasses down from my head to cover my eyes. At least I can try to hide the fact I'm staring if they catch me.

Maddox, the one I've had the pleasure of encountering on multiple occasions, is leaning against the side of the car smoking a cigarette and glaring at his phone like it's insulted him. He is the shortest one in the bunch, but he still has to be at least six feet. With his sleeveless black shirt, I am absolutely enjoying the view of his tattoo-covered arms and broad chest. My mouth waters as I take in the rest of his fit body. The thick thighs and juicy ass... His calves have tattoos on them too, and I notice there doesn't seem to be an ounce of color in any of his artwork.

I turn my attention to the tallest of the guys, maybe six-three, six-four? He's leaner than the others, but his body is defined. His faded red t-shirt hugs his body nicely, and he fills out the Dickies shorts he's wearing nicely. The red Converse on his feet says a lot about his personality. I bet he has them in multiple colors. His hair is dirty blonde and pulled into a messy bun at the back of his head. I wonder how long it is? A stray piece keeps falling into his eyes, and he tucks it behind his ear over and over, like this is normal for him. He's the only one doing anything of importance, picking up bags and loading them into the trunk. I wonder what it is they are doing here and where they are going. They have a lot of bags for just a few nights' stay.

The third guy is sitting on a parking bumper in the spot beside where their Jeep is parked. His hair is a light golden brown in a fashionable combover. It looks so soft and smooth, like he takes a lot of time on his appearance. Black framed glasses rest on his straight nose, and he has a pointed chin that makes him look like he could be a model... maybe he is a model. He's also not as muscled as Maddox, but he's a little thicker than the tall one. He fits nicely into the light, expensive-looking jeans he's wearing. Yeah, I'm definitely drooling at this point.

The last guy looks like he has a stick up his ass. He's bald, with a dark brown beard, the sun showing off the bits of red highlights in it. There is a tattoo on the back of his head, but I can't make out what it is from here. He also has tattoos covering his entire left arm and hand, though they're bright and colorful, the complete opposite of Maddox's. His build is similar to Maddox's, wide and muscular. He's dressed simply in cargo shorts and a gray t-shirt. The scowl on his face though... he looks like he's angry at the world, like he's one of those guys who wouldn't even bother looking at you because you aren't worth his time.

What an interesting group of guys...

I find myself biting my lip as I watch them. They're a really nice distraction from the shit my life has become. But distractions aren't what I need right now. I can't live in a fantasy world because reality is crashing down on me, and hard. I drop the bag to the cement, and then head inside to grab another. I kneel down to tie it, then pull it toward the door. This one is much heavier than the last. Hopefully it won't tear open. When I get outside this time, I catch Maddox staring at me from across the lot, but I pretend I don't notice it.

It's too late though. Something draws me to him, and I turn my head, making eye contact. I stare a little too long, and he starts to walk toward me.

Shit.

What am I supposed to do now? I duck my head and drop the bag. It lands on my foot, and I tug it out harshly, causing me to lose my balance and stumble. I catch myself and hurry around the bag, trying to make it inside before he reaches me, but it's too late. He's there, right by my door, that smirk on his lips that are just so tempting.

"Did you enjoy your food?" He smiles a gorgeous smile that has my heart fluttering in my chest. I quickly clear my throat and respond.

"I threw it out," I lie, leaning against the cool brick of the building, pursing my lips.

"You're lying," he says matter-of-factly. I narrow my eyes at him.

"What do you want?" I ask, trying to sound bored. My heart is picking up in my chest and my palms are growing sweaty.

"Come with us."

I do everything in my power to hide the shock I feel. I clench my jaw and fists, worried I'll jump into his arms and beg him to take me away. Go with them? Why does that sound so appealing? Why do I want to? I don't even know them, and I've spent every chance trying to ignore his advances, but now, suddenly, I just want to go?

"No," I manage to choke out, but I regret it instantly. I want to go with him. I want to take off with four hot and strange men, start a new life, and forget about my current one that is full of nothing but bullshit. I find myself pleading that he fights this, that he asks me again, that he pushes me to do this.

God, Friday, why do you have to be so damn stubborn?
I wish I knew.

"Why not? It's not like you have anything here. I overheard your conversation with that red-headed dork. The one with the puppy dog eyes. He wants in your pants, you know." He smirks.

Fucking cocky is right.

"What's it matter to you who wants to get in my pants?" I plant my hand on my hip and raise a brow. This guy doesn't even know who I am, and he's going to complain about some young guy wanting to fuck me. It's none of his business!

"It doesn't." He scoffs, gives me a once over, and turns to leave.

Fuck, I don't know what to do! He's right, I don't have anything here or anywhere. My life is shit. I don't want to go back to my mother or anywhere near here. What do I have to lose? Besides my life and my limbs? Nothing. I mean, I'm risking my life going back with my mother—she very well could try to kill me. I may as well risk it with these guys who are very hot... I stare at his back as he walks away, my gaze going to his ass. God, it's so nice. I then dart my eyes to the other three guys waiting by the Jeep.

Maddox is halfway across the lot now. I don't have much time.

Fuck it. Fuck it all.

"Wait!" I shout. He stops, turns and meets my eyes, that cocky smile playing across his lips again. He raises a brow, those silvery grey eyes bright in the sunlight. My hands fidget with my shirt and I let out a sigh. "Fine, I'll go, but I need to wait for Todd to g—"

"Put them in the Jeep. We have room."

"You guys just loaded that thing up. They won't fit." I saw the trunk full. The tall guy was shoving them in there.

"Hey, Lenny!" Maddox shouts but keeps his eyes on me.

"Yeah, Mad?" he calls back.

"Open up the back; we got more bags." Lenny nods and opens the trunk door that now looks almost empty, even though I could have sworn it was just full of their stuff. What the hell... "Get over here and help."

Lenny walks over and picks up both my giant bags, one in each hand. I raise a brow, watching him as he walks off like he's holding feathers. I knew he was stronger than he looked. I guess Maddox's idea of Lenny helping is for him to do all of the work? I haven't seen Maddox lift a finger. Bossy motherfucker... but why do I like it? Why do I suddenly have a swarm of butterflies in my stomach? My god, why is his demanding tone doing things to my insides?

I'm certain I'm broken at this point. There's no other explanation.

"What's your name, beautiful?" Maddox asks.

"Friday."

"Well, well, I guess it's *my* lucky Friday, isn't it?" His tone sends unexpected shivers through me, and I ignore the cheesy remark. He takes my hand and pulls me toward their car. His touch sends sparks through me, zapping up my arm and settling in my chest. "Friday, I'd like you to meet the guys. This is Lenny." He points to him, even though I already knew who he was because I have a brain. He waves at me, flashing a boyish grin "The baldy over there is Alec, and this fruitcake is Callan." He lastly points to the guy who looks like a model. He gives me an awkward smile that looks entirely forced. The other one, Alec, doesn't even acknowledge me. I knew he was an asshole. I get vibes from people and they're usually accurate.

"I wish you wouldn't make jokes about people's sexuality. It's rude, Maddox." Callan turns to look at me. "I'm not gay, though I have nothing wrong with anyone being gay. It's nice to meet you." His voice is a smooth timbre, so very calming, even though I hear the bit of disdain behind it over Maddox's comment.

"Yeah, whatever. This is Friday and she's coming with us." Maddox hooks a thumb at me. No one responds to what he says, which seems weird. Wouldn't they have something to say about a random girl joining their little road trip? Maybe they do this kind of thing often? I'm not sure if that thought makes me feel better or worse about getting into their car.

"Callan, get your ass in the back with the other guys. Friday is sitting in front with me. Come on, beautiful." He tugs my arm, bringing me to the front of the car. He stands by the door, waiting for me to get in and closes it once I'm seated. The car smells like a guy. A mix of testosterone and expensive cologne. It's intoxicating. I do my best to not drool all over his leather seats because I have a feeling he'd have something to say about it. He would also probably take it as a compliment, and this guy needs to be moved down a few pegs. I don't need to stroke his ego and make it worse.

The guys in the back are looking at their phones, completely uninterested in the fact that a random girl is joining them wherever it is they are going. I probably should have asked that question before agreeing. Though with the way my life is right now, it doesn't really matter. I didn't want to go anywhere near my mother, and I still don't. Maybe I can make a friendship with these guys and just go where they go. Maybe I can find a job and just start a new life in a new place. It'll be easier if I have friends, that's for sure.

Maddox walks around to the driver's side, gets in, and starts the car. He backs up and presses the button to roll my window down. I look to my right, wondering why he's opening it. I see Todd standing by the motel door labeled with the number seven on it, staring at me with a confused look on his poor freckled face.

"Sorry, nerd, not your lucky day!" Maddox yells out the window and flips him off. A wave of guilt washes over me. I punch Maddox in the arm, making my frustration known.

"Asshole!" I shout at him, and he only chuckles as he closes the window.

"That was not nice, Maddox," Lenny chastises. "Funny but mean." He huffs out a laugh, and when I look back at him, I see his eyes glued to his phone.

"Don't act like you weren't thinking the same thing. I just have the balls to say it." Maddox is turning out to be cockier than I expected. Not too much for me to handle though. He's met his maker. I love when I get the chance to let my inner bitch out.

"We all have balls, thank you very much," Callan adds. His need to reassure that he isn't gay or unequipped has me wondering if he really is gay... or unequipped.

Silence falls over the car as Maddox gets onto the highway. I rest my head back and close my eyes, wondering if this really was a good idea. I mean, I don't know these guys. This is crazy, right? It's absolutely stupid, that's for sure. Yet, I still can't figure out if my other options were better.

"Where are you guys going?" I ask no one in particular, but it's Maddox who answers. He seems to be the talker of the bunch, the leader, and the one who loves attention.

"Dunno yet."

"Huh?"

"We do this every year," Lenny comments. "We get together, drive around aimlessly for three weeks, and never know where we will end up."

"Yeah, *we.* Not random chicks we pick up at shitty motels." I hear Alec's voice for the first time. I'm surprised by how deep and rough it is.

"Alec, no need to be rude to the lady," Callan says nicely.

"Lady? How old do you think I am?" I whirl around, pinning Callan with a stare.

"I was just, uh, I just—"

"I'm kidding, cutie, calm down." I wink and Callan's cheeks blush a tinge of pink. Poor guy. I'm going to have fun with him. Out of the corner of my eye, I catch Maddox sporting another smirk.

Maybe this was a good idea after all.

Chapter Nine

FRIDAY

No one says much of anything during the first hour we're driving. I find myself drifting in and out of sleep, and I really hope I didn't fart or anything. Something about being in a car makes me tired. I think it brings me back to the days of being a kid. A car ride was the only time I had peace and quiet because it was just me and Mom. She didn't like to talk and drive. When I was home, it was anything but quiet. My mother was always having parties, the kind kids shouldn't be at. Under any circumstances. And when there wasn't a party, she had some flavor of the week over. When they weren't fucking *loudly*, they were fighting. Or more like she was getting her ass beat.

"Did you have a good nap, gorgeous?" Waking up to the husky voice is kind of nice...

"No, not really. Your seats suck. When are we stopping?" I groan and ignore his obnoxious pet names... that I kind of like but won't admit to.

"Not for a while, so suck it up. Be grateful I didn't have you squeeze that nice ass of yours in the back." I glance over my shoulder; none of the guys react to his remark.

"I wouldn't have minded that, not one bit," I respond playfully, more to get a reaction from Maddox than anything. Callan looks up and I stare him dead in the eyes and wink. He instantly turns pink. Lenny shakes from his well-contained laughter. His hand moves to his mouth to wipe some invisible thing away, but I know he's trying to hide his smile, not wanting to laugh at the unwanted girl's joke. I'm not offended, I haven't been wanted for most of my life. I can handle it, because the outcome will be good. I'm doing this to get out of a shitty situation. But it's clear Lenny is enjoying my antics as well. Hey, we need some kind of entertainment while on the road. These guys are too grumpy for me.

"Tell me your story, beautiful. What were you doing in that shitty motel by yourself, anyway?" Maddox asks.

"Yeah, Friday. Tell us," Lenny adds, bouncing in his seat and finally putting his phone down.

"You're a jumpy one, aren't you?" I say over my shoulder. I clear my throat before telling them what they want to know. "I caught my boyfriend in bed with another woman, so I took off," I state with a shrug like it's nothing. Because it will be *nothing*. I go on to tell them the rest of it. Everything from my car to Todd—because Maddox seems especially curious about him. Lenny looks genuinely sad for me. Callan is wearing a frown on his face and avoiding eye contact, Alec is still stone-faced. I doubt he was listening at all. I wonder what, if anything, would pull a reaction from him, though. I'll admit, I'm nervous to try. He is not as easy-going as Callan seems to be.

"Someone cheated on you? You're too hot to be cheated on."

Thanks, Maddox, that totally helps.

"Is that even a thing?" Callan chimes in.

"I know, hard to believe, right?" I waggle my eyebrows. But no, it isn't a *thing*.

"What I *mean* is that girls of all levels of 'hotness'"—he uses the finger quotes—"could get cheated on. I don't think looks are taken into consideration when someone decides to be unfaithful," Callan explains.

"You need to get laid, bro," Maddox quips. I bark out a laugh. Looking into the back seat, I see Lenny's face is red from holding in laughter. He finally explodes, his laughter so contagious I can't help but giggle with him.

"Fuck him. He can have fun banging that fake blonde," I add once the laughter calms down. "I don't need him or his dirty dick. Who knows what other broads he was fucking behind my back?"

I was worried about having an STD, because it's true—I don't know how many other people he has cheated on me with. Could have been only her or it could have been many others. Luckily, I had my annual exam a month ago and everything was clean. We hadn't had sex since. Part of me wants to go again, and maybe I will, once I find a place to settle in. If only to ease my mind. I could have asked him, but I doubt he'd tell me the truth.

"Broads? I love it." Lenny snickers and slaps his leg. He's so happy-go-lucky. His laughter and excitement are like a breath of fresh air to me. These little conversations alone are already making me feel better about the awful situation I'm in. I guess it really is true—laughter heals the soul.

"What happened, exactly?" Callan asks as he pushes his glasses up the bridge of his nose using his pointer finger, somehow making the simple motion look really fucking sexy. I find myself biting my bottom lip, my thoughts going somewhere they shouldn't be.

"I was out shopping, got back home, and found him with a blonde attached to his dick. Apparently, he thought he could sneak in a quickie while I was out. Guess he wasn't quick enough." I purse my lips as I replay the scene in my head. "They worked together for like, a year or something. I always got a weird vibe from her, but it happens a lot with girls, so I ignored it. It took them a while to realize I was there watching them… ya know, when I found them? It was like a car accident. You don't want to look, but you also can't look away." I shake my head and a shiver courses through me.

"When dickhead realized I was there, he pushed her off him so hard she bounced off the bed and fell onto the floor. Which, now that I think about it, is actually hilarious." I twist a few loose strands of hair around my fingers as I talk. "He gets up from the bed, dick flopping all over the place as he comes up to me, apologizing, giving me the cliché story of 'it wasn't what it looked like,' yadda, yadda, yadda. In the moment, I felt nothing. I didn't react. I was in shock, I guess. I grabbed an outfit, one that would make my ass look amazing, these skintight jeans and a pair of red heels with a black blouse. He always liked my ass, just apparently not enough. I hopped in the shower, got dressed—"

"Wait, wait… you took a *shower*? With the girl still there?" Lenny asks, leaning forward. His eyes wide with disbelief, jaw on the floor.

"Yep. I wanted him to see what he was missing out on. When I got out of the shower, she was gone, though."

"That's fucking epic," Lenny says.

"Anyway, when I was done getting dressed, everything finally hit me. I threw a bunch of my stuff in garbage bags while he followed me around like a lost puppy dog. It became so annoying

I whipped my phone at him. Lucky for him, I missed. I'm sure it would have knocked out a tooth. It hit the wall and shattered my screen to the point of no return. I just got this one"—I wave my new phone in front of me—"yesterday."

Everyone but Alec is listening intently, or maybe he is but is pretending he isn't. Callan and Lenny have their eyes glued to me. Alec is still staring down at his phone, his face blank, and Maddox keeps giving me looks out of the corner of his eye. I turn in my seat toward Maddox so I can see easily into the back seat.

"I took off with our beater car. It died on the highway like five miles from Ellbrooke, so I walked to the motel and that's when you guys found me."

"You walked five miles down the highway *in heels*?" Lenny asks, staring at me with wide eyes.

"Yeah, my feet were on *fire*. It was awful. I'm still paying for it." I cringe at the thought of how badly my feet still ache.

"Wow, Friday, I'm sorry to hear that. He does not sound like an upstanding guy." Callan shakes his head slowly, fixing his glasses once again.

"Nah, he's an asshat. Wasted four years of my life. He could have broken up with me, ya know? And I would have been fine with it. I don't think I've loved him for a while now. Well, I guess I love him, but I haven't been *in love* with him for a long time. Still, walking in on some girl riding my boyfriend is not how I wanted my relationship to end."

"Ouch. Yeah, I can see that being rough," Callan says.

"You want me to kick his ass?" Maddox grunts out.

"Thanks, but no thanks. My ignoring him is torture, trust me. I know him, and the longer I ignore him, the worse it is. Especially because I took off and he has no idea where I am. I have no family or anything around where we lived, so he has no idea where I could be. That alone is driving him batshit crazy.

He probably expected me to be back by now." It's the truth. I know him well enough to know what drives him crazy and what doesn't. Not knowing is the worst for him. He'd always get upset when he didn't know where I was.

"Has he been texting you?" Maddox asks.

I almost don't answer that because it's none of his business. Why does he care who texts me or doesn't? I could go back to my cheating boyfriend if I wanted, and he wouldn't have a say in the matter. But I do answer because it's nice to talk to someone. It's nice to feel like someone cares, like someone wants to know my story.

"Yeah, but not as much recently. When I first got the new phone it was bad, but—"

"You tell me if he keeps bothering you and I will take care of it." Maddox's statement should spark some concern, right? I don't know this guy, why should he care? Is this one of those red flags people always talk about? Damn, there were about a million of those with shithead I should have paid attention to... the fact that Maddox's comment doesn't spark concern is what concerns me. The fact that it causes my insides to warm with want, now *that* is just fucked.

Callan's sweet, honey-like voice pulls me out of my thoughts. I like how interested he seems.

"How far did you live from Ellbrooke?"

"I was driving for about ten hours, I think."

"And you don't have family there? Where are they?" Callan asks. The more he talks, the stronger his voice becomes, like he's more comfortable.

"Nope, and not anywhere I care to be. I was going to go back home, if that's what you want to call it, but it's pointless. My mother is a bigger shithead than my ex, if you can believe that. She's really the only family I have. So, if your plan is to kill me, you'll probably get away with it." I turn my head to look out the window.

Dead silence. Shit, I was at least expecting *something* from Maddox.

"Guys... I'm kidding. I don't think you're trying to kill me. Jeez, lighten up." I roll my eyes and catch my smirk in the reflection of the window. These guys are too easy to mess with.

Chapter Ten

FRIDAY

A few very long and tiring hours later, we pull off the highway with plans to stop for a night or two. We've stopped only once since leaving Ellbrooke to gas up and pee, and it was very quick. I barely had time to stretch, though my body was grateful for the short walk from the car to the bathroom. I tried to take my time, but Maddox was shouting at me from the car to hurry up, so I didn't have much of a choice. He's very bossy and I hate how much I like it. He sounds like an asshole, but somewhere deep down I know he isn't doing it to be cruel, he's just trying to keep everything from falling apart. He's keeping us in line to make sure we get to where we need to go. But his tone? My god, his tone is something else.

The sign at the end of the exit reads *Bradbury*. While we're stopped at the faded and dented stop sign, I notice this town looks similar to the last one we were in. It has that small town feel to it. Lots of land, small buildings, and not congested with cars or people.

"You guys have a thing for small towns, huh?" I cock an eyebrow at Maddox. The three guys in the back are all passed out. Lenny's head is leaning against the headrest, mouth wide open. Is that... is that drool? I shake my head. Alec and Callan have their heads resting on their arms that are against the doors, both sleeping peacefully. This is why they aren't the ones who drive... plus Maddox has control issues. He only admitted the first part of that. The second part I figured out on my own.

"We're from a big city. Part of the vacation excitement is getting away from it," Callan answers in a sleepy voice, adding to the sexiness of it. I shoot him a look and his eyes are still closed. I look to Maddox and mouth the words *sleep talking?* He shrugs in response. We drive for roughly ten more minutes until we reach a motel. We would have been here sooner, but the GPS was lagging due to the lack of signal. Normally, being off the grid would stress me out, but now? I am looking forward to my phone not blowing up.

The motel is small and in the shape of an L. It has only one floor, the seemingly once bright green paint is now dark, dull, and faded. The open sign above the office reads "pen", the "O" not working. No one seems to care enough to fix it, or anything else around this place. We pull into a parking spot by the office door and Maddox kills the engine. He gets out of the car. Maybe I checked his ass out as he stepped out... maybe I didn't. He pops his head back in before shutting the door. "Stay here, I'll be right back."

Where the fuck would I go? Where would any of us go?

I turn in my seat to face the guys in the back. Lenny and Alec are still passed out. Callan is doing something on his phone. A game, maybe? I can't really make it out.

"Why so quiet?" I try to start a conversation with Callan. I figure if I'm going to spend time with them, I should get on good terms. It'll make whatever this is a better experience.

"I'm claustrophobic and being stuffed back here is bothersome. Normally, I'm quite talkative." His voice is lacking emotion, and his eyes are not leaving the phone.

"Not when it comes to girls," Lenny mumbles under his breath so quietly I barely hear it. Is he awake or talking in his sleep? If he's insulting him in his sleep, that is funny on an entirely new level.

"I'm sorry, why didn't you tell me? I would have sat back there," I say, feeling really bad about this. Maddox is a dick. I'm sure he knew. *He* should have said something. This isn't the type of first impression I want to give these guys. I'm not trying to impose or make any of them uncomfortable. I hope they don't think that.

"Maddox's orders. Besides, I was trying to be a gentleman. I'm fine." He waves his hand at me, dismissing my guilt.

I turn back around and turn the volume up on the radio. I flip through stations while waiting for Maddox to come out. There aren't many working stations, which doesn't surprise me because of the lack of cell signal. Maddox returns a few minutes later, two key rings dangling from his fingers. Great, I wonder who I'll be sharing a room with. Knowing the little bit I know about these guys so far, I know it won't be Alec, probably not Callan either. Most likely Maddox and Lenny. The thought of spending the night in the same room with both of them sends heat pooling to my belly. The things that could happen... Nope, not going there! I can't.

Maddox gets back into the car, lowers the radio volume, and drives toward the end of the lot, parking in the last spot. He gets out of the car first and comes around to open the door for me. This time, I beat him to it. I like him trying to be all gentleman-like, but I can't let it get to his head. He offers me his hand to help me out and I give in. Mostly because I want to feel his hands. He's a right cocky asshole, but he really is sweet. It's frustrating. I want to punch him and fuck him at the same time. Maybe he's into that... A girl can dream, right?

That's it, I must have truly lost my mind. That fuckwad messed me up more than I thought. What am I doing right now? I got into a car with four guys. Four *random* guys I have never met before. Now, here I am, thinking about fucking them. Well, only one. Maybe two. But fuck, still! That's not right. I need to kick it back a bit, tone it down a notch, and take some time to think about what happened. Obviously, I'm upset. It hasn't hit me yet... why is it taking so long? Why don't I feel sad? I feel... fine. Like nothing ever happened. Like I didn't walk in on my boyfriend fucking someone else. Like this is where I belong, this is where I am supposed to be. That's weird, right? I guess it could be because I didn't love him anymore, so it isn't bothering me. That's a possibility. I was angry at first, but it was because he was a dick about the situation. Not because I was sad. The fact that life has royally kicked my ass and left me on the ground with nothing but skinned knees *should* be upsetting me. But it's not.

Fuck it. You only live once, right? *Right.*

With that, I take his hand, allowing him to help me the rest of the way out of the car. My hand tingles with his touch as he leads me to the last motel door on the right. I move to the side while he unlocks it, eyeing the barren parking lot. There isn't anything here other than this motel and trees. I get these are small towns, but it's summer. Shouldn't there be more people staying at these places? Is this going to be the last thing I see before they kill me?

Swinging the door open and putting the stopper down, Maddox walks back to the car, pulling out a cigarette from the pack he keeps in his pocket. I walk into the dark room, swiping at the wall for the light switch. As the light flicks on, my eyes go wide as I take in the room in front of me. *Holy shit.*

There are two queen beds both covered in white, fluffy comforters with dark red accent pillows thrown about. There is a long dresser across from the beds and a bedside table between them, which are made of dark stained wood. In the corner is a small desk and chair made of the same wood. The opposite corner has a small white fridge placed underneath a shelf that is holding a microwave. Above the dresser is a mounted flat-screen TV larger than the one I had at home. There are abstract paintings hanging on the walls, the color scheme matching the rest of the décor. Directly across from me is another door that must lead to the bathroom, which I am now very curious to see. This is not what I was expecting when driving into this place.

Moving quickly to see the bathroom, I find it's just as pleasing. I let out a sigh of relief. After dealing with the bathroom in the last place, I am thanking the universe for this. This one is all white with a large tub and shower combo to the left. Nothing spectacular, but it's also bigger than the one I had at home. In the center is a gray countertop, with a porcelain sink and a large mirror. The toilet is off to the right behind a privacy wall. There is a shelf in the corner filled with towels and toiletries. I am speechless. Never in a million years would I have expected this place to look like this on the inside. A hidden gem. Amazing.

As I exit the bathroom, Maddox and Lenny come strolling in. Lenny is carrying my trash bags and Maddox is carrying two backpacks that I assume are his and Lenny's. I mentally high-five myself being right about who I'd be sharing a room with. I love when I'm right, even if I'm the only one who knows about it. Lenny drops the bags against the wall by the bathroom, and Maddox places his on the side of the bed. He walks over to the adjoining door that I didn't notice, unlocks, and opens it. He walks in and I hear him tell someone, probably Callan because

I don't think he would order Alec around like that, to order food because we're staying in for the night. The more he bosses people around, the hotter it gets. Yeah, something is definitely wrong with me. Maybe *I'm* the one who needs to get laid. How long has it been? A month? Two? I've lost track. Possibly longer than that. Ouch. It was never worth remembering, that's the first problem.

Maddox comes back through the door, pulling his shirt over his head and dropping it on the floor.

My eyes rake over his chest, and it's like time slows down. I take in every curve of muscle, every dip and line across his stomach and chest. Yeah, I definitely need to get laid. *By that.*

His eyes meet mine, fire burning in his silver irises, and a cocky smirk on his full lips. One that makes the butterflies in my stomach go crazy. I know I said I didn't want to make his head big, but damn, he has a really nice body. His arms and broad chest are covered in ink and chiseled with muscles. Everything on him looks so... firm. Yet, his skin looks so soft and smooth. I catch myself biting my lip and quickly stop. I have to mentally slap myself because I know he knows I am ogling him. I'm one hundred percent positive it went straight to his head. Dammit, and I was trying so hard not to do that... but it's so hard, his body is just so tempting.

He turns and walks into the bathroom without a word. The muscles in his back ripple as he goes. He leaves the door open an inch, and it's probably an invitation, but I don't give in that easily. If he were in front of me, it'd be hard to say no. Now that he's gone, the lust fog has dissipated. But the moisture between my legs hasn't.

I know I've said it, but it needs to be said again. I'm *really* going to get myself into serious trouble with these guys. I run my hand down my face and blow out a breath. I need to get it together. The attraction I feel toward him is simply because he's exactly my type, a type I've always been attracted to but rarely got to be with. My asshole ex had zero tattoos and half the muscles of Maddox. He was decent looking, but nowhere near as hot as these guys.

"Friday. That's a cool name. Where did it come from?" Lenny asks, leaning against the dresser with his legs crossed at the ankles. Honestly, I didn't realize he was still here. My focus was purely on the half-naked Adonis that I'll be sharing a room with. I hope he didn't see me drooling over Maddox. That would be embarrassing. I turn toward him and try to pull my thoughts to somewhere safe.

"My mom swore she got knocked up on a Friday, thought it would be funny," I say with a shrug. It really is as simple as that. No crazy back story, no special meaning. Just a mother so high, the only name she thought of for her child was a day of the week.

"Ah, yeah that's, uhm... I don't know what to say to that." He scratches his head and shifts on his feet. Poor guy looks so uncomfortable.

"It's just a name, I'm not offended." I try to make him feel better. There's no need to be uncomfortable. I've accepted the shit I've been handed in life. I don't lose sleep over it. It's just a name. Not something to cry about.

Pushing off the dresser, he sits next to me on the bed. The side of me that's closest to him starts to tingle, almost to the point of itchiness. I furrow my brows and look up to meet his bright blue eyes for just a moment. He has a similar confused expression on his face and his hand goes to his arm as he rubs it and stands up, looking a little freaked out. Did he feel it too? That would be weird right? The attraction I feel toward him can't possibly be felt in return, can it?

"I'm gonna go hang out with the guys over there. You can come if you want," he says as he shoves his hands into his pockets, rocking back on his heels.

"I think I'll stay here. I have a feeling they don't like me very much." I slip out of my shoes and kick them toward the wall, where they roll a few times before stopping.

Lenny bends down and I catch a much better glimpse of his eyes. They are a beautiful shade of blue. Dark but bright, with a light, almost silver ring around the center, like the ocean glimmering in the sun. He gets so close, I think he's going to kiss me, the butterflies in my belly go crazy once again. But instead of moving forward, he goes to my side, his cheek brushing mine as he whispers words into my ear, goosebumps erupting over my flesh. This time, I'm not sure if it's from him being next to me, or from how turned on I got from thinking he was going to kiss me.

"Alec is a dick and doesn't like anyone. Callan is not good with women." He brushes his lips across my ear lobe before backing up and watching me curiously, his eyes filled with heat.

"And you are?" I choke the words out, my voice betraying me.

"I'll let you be the judge of that." He winks and disappears into the other room, leaving me alone, clenching my thighs... over what, words?

I really need to get laid.

I plop back on the bed, my hand going to the side of my face that's burning from his touch. Why does that happen when he gets so close? I know I haven't had sex in a while, but there is no way my body is reacting like *that*. I've gone longer before. Maybe my hormones are out of whack from stress. Yeah, let's go with that.

The bathroom door opens, pulling me from my thoughts. Maddox walks out in nothing but a white towel wrapped loosely around his narrow waist. The steam from the shower swirls out of the doorway behind him as the heat mixes with the cold air of the room. He reaches for one of the black backpacks he carried in, picks it up, and puts it on the bed. He digs through it in search of something to wear. I'm staring at him, but he hasn't looked at me once. *Cocky motherfucker.* He pulls out a pair of *grey* sweatpants, dropping them on the bed. Fucking great. That is not what I need right now. I'm having enough trouble keeping my mind out of the gutter and he has to go and put on *grey sweatpants*? Lord, help me.

He puts his bag back on the floor and turns to me, matching my look. His dark and stormy eyes are like nothing I have ever seen before. Like the sky when a rainstorm is coming in. I notice now they're more silver than grey. A sly grin moves across his lips as he allows the towel to fall to the floor. It takes everything in me to not look down.

Don't do it, Friday, don't do it!

Fuck... I did it.

Holy shit, that thing? Damn, that thing is *big.*

Much bigger than the one I had at home.

I can't imagine what it looks like when it's erect. I swallow *hard*, quickly looking back up at Maddox's face, to realize his grin has grown bigger and cockier. Get it? *Cock*-ier.

He takes his sweatpants from the bed and slowly—seductively, even—pulls them on. Fuck, it is working. He knows exactly what he is doing and fuck me for not being able to resist. I may need a new pair of panties. It's possible the bed beneath me is soaked.

I'd be lying if I said I haven't thought about fucking them. Alone and together. I've never been with more than one person at a time, but I'm not opposed to it. Actually, it's a fantasy, and if these guys wanted to do it, I would have no objections. Please, take me.

A knock sounds on the door from the other room. A moment passes and Callan greets the delivery guy. A few moments later, the smell of pizza fills the air and my mouth waters. I haven't had much to eat the last few days and pizza sounds delicious.

"Let's go." Maddox takes my hand and pulls me into the other room, not giving me an option of whether I want to go or not. As I follow, my eyes stay on his arm, taking in the thick muscles and how I want to touch them.

My panties are getting wetter by the minute.

Lenny and Callan are sitting Indian style on the bed closest to us, Alec is sitting in a small wooden chair stationed in front of the desk. This room is a mirror image of the other, but instead of the dark red accents, this room has navy blue popping up all over. Maddox pulls me toward the bed and sits, pulling me down with him, making me fall over onto his lap. Maddox slaps my ass, then pushes me upright.

Handsy piece of shit! I should shout at him, should tell him to fuck off, but I don't. I just sit and act like it didn't happen.

Lenny hands one of the three boxes of pizza over to Maddox, the smell instantly eradicating my anger. The box of greasy, cheesy deliciousness ends up between Maddox and me. I immediately reach for the box and grab two slices of cheese before I'm even handed a plate.

"How long are we staying here?" I ask between bites.

"A few days," Maddox answers.

"You talk a lot," I retort.

"He likes the sound of his own voice," Lenny says.

I snort out a laugh, nearly choking on my food. I quickly swallow and take a sip of water that was handed to me. The bottle is warm, but it's better than nothing.

"It's not my fault I have a nice voice," Maddox responds. He's right though; he does. He notices me staring, my emotions written on my face, and he winks. Fucking fuck, this guy. He slides the box of pizza out of the way and gets nose to nose with me. His spicy scent hits my nose, overthrowing the smell of bread and cheese and sauce. "And there are plenty of other things I can do with my mouth I know you will enjoy." He moves back to his spot and continues to eat his pizza as if what he said didn't just literally take my breath away. Not in a romantic way, but in the holy-shit-I-want-to-fuck-you kind of way. It takes me a moment to get myself together, but once I do, I focus on eating. Nothing else.

After finishing both slices, I grab another... and then another.

By the time we're done, we've demolished three large pizzas. Not surprised with the number of guys here; they all look like they can eat quite a bit. Plus, it's pizza. Everyone always eats too much pizza.

"I'm gonna call it a night, guys. I'm mentally exhausted and could really use some sleep." That, and I'm not up for conversation or trying to be nice anymore. I don't want them to get the wrong idea of me because I'm cranky. They all say their goodnights, except for Alec, who ignores me as usual. I don't know how long I'm going to be with these guys, but trust me when I say I will break that man wide open before we part ways. As I enter back into my room, I pull the door closed after me, leaving it open just an inch. I get comfy in my panties and camisole and get into the bed, throwing only the thin top sheet over me. The air conditioner hasn't kicked in yet, so it's warm in here. Plus, being surrounded by hot guys? I need to cool down.

CHAPTER ELEVEN

FRIDAY

The feeling of someone crawling into bed rouses me from a deep sleep. This bed is much more comfortable than the last and I fell asleep so quickly. The air conditioner in this room works better than the last too, and it's now chilled. I always sleep better in a cold room. I assume it's Maddox who woke me since he thinks he can do whatever he wants, and I'm too tired to care who it is. I roll over, expecting to tell Maddox off, but when I open my eyes, there are a pair of bright blue eyes staring down at me, attached to someone who is wearing nothing but a flattering pair of boxer briefs. *Lenny.*

"What are you doing?" I ask in a sleepy whisper, not knowing if any of the other guys are around and not wanting to wake them if they are. It feels late, or really early.

Lenny bends down, hovering over me. "Showing you how good I can be," he whispers against my mouth.

Before I can muster up a response, his lips are on mine. He kisses me hard, but slow. I feel his need through his lips. His hands press into the pillow beside my head as he climbs on top of me, his skin hot against mine. His excitement pressing against my center. His hand moves from the bed and down to my hip, squeezing my flesh. He pulls me up, pressing me into him, making him harder and me wetter. The feel of him between my legs causes me to moan into his mouth. It probably should bother me that three other guys are here... somewhere, but it doesn't. Instead, it turns me on *more*. It's exciting knowing we could be caught. Or better yet, *joined*. My entire body heats as his hands slide over me, the soft moans coming from him making me want him even more.

I tell myself I should not be doing this. I know I shouldn't... but I can't help it. For some reason I cannot explain, I want this. I want *him*.

His fingers slide under my shirt and brush against my skin, the soft feel of his fingertips causes goosebumps as he pulls my shirt up, freeing my breasts. His hand cups one and he rolls my hardened nipple through his fingers, drawing yet another moan from my lips. His mouth moves down to my nipple, taking it between his lips and sucking gently. He trails down my belly, to my hip, placing hot kisses as he goes. He pauses for a moment, sitting back on his heels with a look on his face that I can only describe as contemplative.

My chest heaves as I wait for him to make a move, wanting him to keep going but unable to say the words. He steps off the bed, pulls his briefs down and then climbs back up, settling between my legs once again. His mouth returns to my hip for a short moment before he brings his mouth over my pussy. His hot breath causes my hips to lift and push into his mouth. Only the thin material of my soaked panties keeps his tongue from touching the sensitive flesh between my legs. The heat of his mouth has me pressing into him, the pressure of his lips and mouth on me has me aching for more.

His fingers dig into my hips as my hands grab and pull at the sheets. His mouth continues over me and it's taking everything in me to not yell at him to take off my panties so I can feel his tongue on me. *Fuck.* He must feel my frustration because he mumbles a word that I barely hear due to his mouthful of pussy.

Patience.

I barely make it out.

No. No fucking patience. I don't have any, and I don't want any. What I want is his mouth on me, making me come.

He does this for a while, teasing and building me up to orgasm and then backing off. When he finally pulls my panties down, I swear I cry out in relief. Yes! Fucking finally! He moves on top of me, placing his hands on the bed on either side of my head. The plump tip of his cock slides up and down my wet crease and stops at my entrance. He moves his hips slightly, causing his hard cock to move up and rub over my clit once again. I buck against him.

"You want this?" He grabs his cock by the base, still rubbing it over my entrance and swirling it around my clit.

"Yes, I do." My hands are on his hips, pulling him to me, but he doesn't budge.

He keeps up this game a little longer. Teasing me to the point of madness. Just when I think he's done and he's going to fuck me, he backs off. Bringing his mouth back down, he dives into me, lapping up all the wetness he just created between my legs.

Fuck. Yes.

But how the hell does he have so much damn self-control?

I mumble words between moans and groans. Some are indistinguishable. Most, actually. It doesn't take him long to build me up again, but when I get close, he stops. Gods, it's so frustrating.

He likes games.

Asshole.

He waits long enough for me to come back down before going at it again. I'm getting frustrated. At the same time, this is so fucking hot. Most guys I've been with are not this into pleasing me. None of them have ever taken time with me like this. Not to tease me, not to please me. Nothing. It's straight to the point. Of course I've had guys go down on me but never *for me.* Not like this. My eyes hurt from being screwed shut for far too long, I open them wanting to get a look at Lenny with a mouthful of me. But when I open them, I see something unexpected... some*one*, actually.

Maddox is standing in the doorway. Watching. The light from the TV illuminates his sharp features. He's leaning on the door jamb, wearing only his sweatpants. The bulge in his pants tells me he likes what he sees. Lenny has no idea someone is watching, but the scene in front of me almost pushes me over the edge. My hands twist in Lenny's hair, pushing his face harder into my pussy, adding more pressure from his tongue. The pressure that I so desperately need to get me what I want. My eyes stay locked on Maddox, and I run my tongue along my bottom lip, biting down on it. His hand moves down, and he grabs his cock through his pants, slowly dragging it up and down, allowing me to see how hard he really is. This causes an almost embarrassing sound to leave my throat. Maddox slips his pants down slowly and steps out of them. Gripping his cock, he walks toward the bed and pauses behind Lenny before grazing his hand ever so gently over Lenny's back and down his hip.

For a moment, I worry Lenny is going to freak and I will never get this orgasm I desperately fucking need. Of course I could do it myself, but I really don't want to. Lenny hesitates for a second, but just as quickly as he falters, he starts right back up again, licking from my opening back up to my clit. Maddox stands behind him still gripping his cock, slowly stroking himself, his other hand placed on Lenny's hip. He steps back, bending down to grab something out of one of the bags on the floor. When he stands, I see a small bottle in his hand that I can only assume is lube.

He moves back to his spot behind Lenny, never taking his eyes from mine. He pours the clear liquid into his hand, slathering it onto his thick hardness. He pours more into his hand and this time he rubs it onto Lenny. I feel the vibration of a moan come from Lenny's mouth as Maddox uses a finger on him. I'm doing everything I can to hold back the orgasm, but it isn't easy. As much as I want it, I don't want this to end. I need to keep watching, need to see what's going to happen. The anticipation has my stomach swirling with lust. Lenny is enjoying himself, and fuck, I want to see Maddox take Lenny right in front of me.

Maddox lines up behind him and slowly pushes in with a low growl. Lenny pulls away from my pussy only long enough to let out a short breathy moan. His eyes are closed but his face is filled with what I think is pain, but quickly realize is pleasure.

This isn't their first time, I think. This all seems too easy for this to have never happened before. Lenny is too accepting of it, too willing. Do they do this often?

Lenny takes his finger and slides it over my opening, entering me slowly, adding another finger after feeling me out. The fullness of his fingers in me is so right and I push myself into him, needing more. Lenny and Maddox both keep their eyes trained on me. My head rolls back in pleasure. As much as I want to keep their gaze, I can't. Lenny's fingers move faster and faster. When he adds his tongue, I'm done for. The orgasm is right there, getting closer and closer. My body tingles and heats, my muscles clenching.

Maddox continues his movements, going harder. So hard, the skin-to-skin slapping sound fills the silence. His pounding causes Lenny to jerk into me. My hips move off the bed as I grind into his mouth. Feeling Maddox fuck Lenny is what pushes me over the edge and the orgasm takes over my body. I cry out as my body convulses under Lenny's tongue. My back arches and my grip tightens on the sheets as I ride out the wave of one of the most intense orgasms I have ever had.

My eyes flick to Maddox when I can get them open, his heated eyes meet mine as he continues to fuck Lenny from behind. His fingers dig into Lenny's hips, holding him still. I catch movement, my eyes instinctively moving to it, and I find Lenny reaching down to stroke himself.

Holy fuck...

I am taken aback by the scene in front of me. So much that I don't know what to do. This is easily the hottest fucking thing that I have ever witnessed in my entire existence. I am so turned on, yet I'm still so sensitive from that intense orgasm I don't know if I could handle being touched again. But I want him to. God, I want Lenny's mouth on me again.

"You like watching me fuck him?" Maddox asks in his deep, husky voice.

Words don't come out, but I manage a nod as I bite my bottom lip, my pussy aching to be filled.

Maddox's movements become faster, more erratic. Lenny's hand is still around his cock, pumping it from base to tip.

"Fuck," he groans. "Mad, I'm gonna come."

Holy fuck. Holy fucking fuck!

Before I can begin to process what is happening right in front of my eyes, wet, hot liquid hits my calf. I look down to see Lenny's seed pumping out all over me and the bed. Maddox stills, releasing himself into Lenny's ass with a groan, his head falling back on his shoulders. I lean up on my elbows, staring because it's all I can do. All too quickly Maddox backs away, snatches his pants from the ground, and disappears into the other room. Lenny crawls onto the bed and lays down beside me. My entire body is tingling, on fire.

"What was that all about?" I ask, still trying to catch my breath and feeling a little confused over the entire ordeal.

"He doesn't like to admit he likes my ass." Lenny shrugs and closes his eyes, resting his hand on his belly. His cock is still semi-hard and part of me wants to take it in my mouth... "Really, he doesn't want other people knowing he likes fucking me."

"This has happened before?" I ask, wanting to know their history.

"A few times." He winks at me, tapping my leg. "Come on, D. Let's go shower." He sits up and heads toward the bathroom.

"D?" I question.

"Yeah, it's your new nickname. Hope you like it."

"Do I have a choice?"

"Nope." I roll my eyes and stand to follow Lenny into the shower.

Showering with Lenny is fun, yet uneventful. I was kind of hoping to get a bit more action in the shower. I don't know why I've suddenly become insatiable for a man I've just met, but I'm not upset about it. I'm beginning to see that anything involving Lenny is fun. He's the life of the party, the one who likes jokes, pranks, and good times. He makes me feel young again.

While in the shower, Lenny washes every inch of me in the most gentle way. He takes his time, quietly humming to himself. An act that should be awkward due to being extremely personal, but in no way, shape, or form did it feel that way. It felt right and normal. Like this is something we've done a hundred times before. When that's done, he washes and conditions my hair. He sings to me the entire time, making me laugh so hard tears pour down my face and my stomach cramps. He belts out some made-up song about taking showers and washing up.

Bubbles bubbles everywhere,
And not a one to spare.
Washing up Friday's hair,
Then she'll get her underwear!

When we get out, he helps me dry off and then we get dressed. As I'm lying in bed beside him, the silly words run through my head, making me laugh quietly. He's snoring softly beside me and he's adorable when he sleeps. There's this boyish glint about him. He looks so innocent and sweet. Maybe getting into the car with these guys was a good idea. They seem like good guys, genuinely nice people, even Alec who has been ignoring me, but at least he's allowing me to be here. I don't think they realize how much they're helping me out by letting me tag along. This could be life changing for me. I owe them a thank you.

I lay awake for a while, unable to sleep from the adrenaline that's still pulsing through my veins over what happened just a short time ago. The image of Maddox fucking Lenny is not something I'll be able to forget for a long time. Not that I want to. The way Maddox just left though, that's kind of an asshole move. He just uses Lenny and then leaves? Is it always like that or did he do it because of me? I make a mental note to ask Lenny about it because that's not sitting right with me. You can't just use people like that. Especially your friends... or are they *together*? Something else I need to ask, but even more of a reason to figure out what the hell is going on. As someone who's been in more horrible relationships than not, I know that was a jerk move on Maddox's part. Lenny is so sweet and fun, and

Maddox is rude and abrasive... Would Lenny say something to Maddox if it bothered him? I'm not sure, which is why I want more information. I'll tell Maddox off if I need to. I've done it enough times already, what's one more?

I roll onto my side to get comfy. A moment later, Lenny's arm slips around my waist and he pulls me close to him. The warmth of his body and his strong arm holding me tight draws me into a deep sleep so quickly.

CHAPTER TWELVE

MADDOX

After last night, I am positive she is our missing mate. I'd bet my left nut on it. And I'm pretty sure Lenny can agree with me at this point. He's not one to sleep around—at all. I'm the one who does that. For him to make a move like that with her... he feels something. It's all still messing with my head though. I can't figure out why the feelings aren't strong. Why isn't the pull toward her more powerful? And why does she act like she can't feel it? Something isn't right, but I know in my gut she belongs to us.

I can't get the thought of Lenny between her legs out of my head. The way he was so into it, touching and teasing her. The sounds she made, how much she wanted him. I felt it, felt her need. The scent of her arousal permeated the air, and my dick grew hard instantly. The moment I knew she saw me, when she watched me watching her and didn't freak out... it only solidified my thoughts on the matter.

Still, I should not have done what I did in front of her. I couldn't help myself; I just needed to be inside him. I wanted her too, but I *needed* him. None of the guys know about Lenny and me, and it needs to stay that way. Granted, it's none of their damn business, but we don't usually keep secrets between us. And this... *relationship* that Lenny and I have? It's something we should tell them, but I know they won't take it well. I told Lenny if he told anyone, I'd kick his ass, and I know he believes me. He can be a real pain in the ass at times, but he has a lot of respect for me. I'm the one who saved him, after all.

I've gone back and forth with what we're doing, trying to decide if it's wrong. I worry that people will think I'm taking advantage of him, but it's not like that. It's never been like that with him. I don't remember when my feelings for him changed; they just did. We're close, we've always been close. More so than the other guys. Plus, it's not unheard of for all mates to be together. It's just that Lenny and I's situation is different than most, but nothing about us has ever gone by the books, why should we start now?

I close the adjoining door fully, so I can talk to the guys alone. It's early in the morning, but most of us like to get an early start. I don't sleep much to begin with, and Lenny sleeps enough for all of us. Waking him up was easy enough; making sure I didn't wake Friday was the tough part. She's sleeping so soundly, looking like a goddamn angel in that bed. Before I woke Lenny, I stood there watching both of them. It just looked right. Seeing them together is *right*.

"How can you be sure it's her?" Alec asks. He's wearing his usual scowl, leaning against the headboard with his arms crossed over his chest. "I haven't felt a damn thing."

I point a finger at Alec. "Quit being such a negative prick and open up, then maybe you will."

"I think Maddox is right. I think she's it," Lenny adds quietly. His eyes are downcast, staring at the floor. I can't tell if he's avoiding an argument or if he's just tired. I knew he felt something, though. I knew it.

"Callan?" I ask as I take a step back and lean against the cool wall.

"I felt *something*, not enough to be sure. But, Maddox, I trust you. You've never led us astray." He lets out a sharp breath. No doubt he's worried about teaming up with me and going against Alec. It shouldn't be that way, but it's how it's been for a long, long time. Alec against Maddox. The sad thing is it never used to be this way. When we were younger, we were as close as two people could be. I went to him for everything. I was the one he called when his life fell apart that night. Me. Now? It's like we don't even know each other.

"It's settled then. She stays. We don't say anything, not yet. She either doesn't know what she is, or she's keeping herself closed off for another reason. I can't tell yet." I run my fingers through my hair as I figure out our next move. I point a finger at Lenny. "And you, chill with the magic shit, she's going to realize something is up."

"Come on, Mad! That's the fun part," he whines.

"I'm serious, Lenny." He pouts and flops down on the bed. I shake my head. "I'm going out for a smoke."

Lenny has always been the kid, the younger brother, the one we have to watch and make sure he doesn't get into trouble. This is why we haven't said anything about us. We're like family, yeah, but it's always been a little more than that with Lenny. It's a touchy subject, and I don't know how I even feel about it. I'm in no way ready to come out to the guys about it. The biggest argument I have is that I'm not the only one who has taken care of him his whole life. We all have. Plus, Lenny is an adult now and can make his own decisions. Still, I could see either Callan or Alec arguing Lenny is incapable of knowing what a healthy relationship looks like due to how he was raised. I think they don't give him enough credit. He may be a certified goofball and entirely immature at times, but he's smart as hell.

I do worry this could be the very thing that sends Alec off the edge. I'm not sure any of us will be able to handle him when that happens. He doesn't react to much, but one of these days, he's bound to. I can't blame him after what happened. He's scarred... broken, entirely fucked up. The shit he endured as a kid, the stuff he saw, especially after that night? What he had to do? It's a lot for anyone. No one would come out of that normal. I'm hoping that finding our mate will bring him back. I miss the old Alec, not this zombie thing that walks around grunting and bitching all day. I just need to make him see that she's it.

We all need this, honestly. We've all had our fair share of bad times, ever since we were kids. It's how we found each other, what brought us together before we knew half the shit we did. It really must have been fate or the universe bringing us together for a specific reason—one I still haven't figured out yet. What are the odds of us all having shitty parents? And not just normal shitty parents, but bottom of the barrel, twisted and fucked in the head parents? *Human* parents. Yet, we found each other at such a young age before we knew what we were.

All of us except Lenny came into our powers around the same time. Either it's because he's younger or something else, I'm not sure. He used to follow us around and pretend he had powers; he wanted to be just like us. It's funny, almost like he knew what he was deep down because he used to pretend to shoot magic out of his fingers. Not that shooting magic out of his fingers is what he does, but he is a warlock. He has magical abilities;

it just took him a long time to figure it out, and even now I think he's still trying to figure it out. But that's what it's like when you have humans for parents, when you don't grow up in a paranormal community. You just have to figure shit out for yourself. Thankfully, the four of us had each other and that certainly made things easier.

The rest of us, all within a few months, noticed something going on. I was the first, always knowing something was off with me from the very beginning. I know there are people out there who like blood and gore; I know it's a relatively normal thing to enjoy a movie or two. My attraction toward it was much different. Even I knew that. It wasn't overbearing, just odd. The feelings and sensations I got over seeing blood were very different than what it should be. Being a vampire is not easy, but it has its perks too. And no, I'm not the bloodthirsty psychopath I thought I'd be. I was petrified at first, especially once my teeth came in, but after some research, my mind was at ease. Plus, Alec was there to help me through it. One of the things I learned about vampires, and a lot of paranormals, is that our blood isn't pure. Not the way it used to be hundreds of years ago. Our blood is so tainted with human blood from paranormals and humans having children, that something as black and white as a vampire isn't so black and white anymore. Almost all paranormals are a gray area, and you don't quite know how you'll turn out until you do. Especially those who come from human parents.

So yeah, I still love blood, especially from the guys, but it's nothing like people think. Not for me, anyway. There are vampires out there who kill to feed, but I'm not one of them. The abilities I have are what I love most. The speed, the strength, the charm, but most of all, becoming invisible. That was the last of my abilities to show, and the one I can't use at will. It's like I'm only allowed to use it so many times. Or maybe I just don't have enough energy to use it as often as I'd like. Either way, it's by far the best thing.

Callan's mind control is intense and extremely rare. He has the ability to manipulate knowledge, which is why he's called a knowledge manipulator. It's possible there's another word for it, but we never found it. We realized when we were young it was extremely dangerous and can really fuck things up. Callan was scared for a long time, and we agreed to help him keep it in check and he agreed to only use it when it was needed. Of course, he still messes with us from time to time, when he's in a goofy mood, but it's never anything dangerous.

We used to stand at street corners and Callan would use his powers on people driving, making them believe red and green were the opposite, but only on one side of traffic. So, people would run a red light, truly thinking it meant it was time to go. We'd laugh at them swerving around each other, yelling and screaming. Until one day, it caused an accident and there was a child in the car. It was scary as fuck, and we felt like complete jackasses. Luckily, everyone was okay, including the child. In a way, I'm grateful for that happening, because without, who knows when we would have stopped. That moment made us realize these gifts were not a joke and they needed to be handled seriously.

Callan was always so well-behaved as a kid. The nerd, the quiet one, the one who never got into trouble. Ever. The accident he caused really scared him. But after that day, he dug into what else he could do with his ability. He spent hours reading books and learning everything he could. He soaks up information like crazy. His brain works like a computer. You ask him something and he can dig through years of information to give you an answer. It's like a puzzle for him, and it's rare for him to not know something at this point. Though, he has learned how to make himself seem more "normal." Callan is not a people person, he doesn't read emotions well, and he's awkward as hell talking to girls, but he at least can have a somewhat normal conversation now without turning it into a study lesson.

And Alec? Gods, Alec... He can be scary as fuck, which is weird coming from me, but I've seen him do some crazy shit when he gets mad. Especially after *that* day. He's an air elemental, and in my opinion, that's the most dangerous of them all. As kids, we thought it was stupid until he started playing around with it and realized what he is truly capable of. He can crush someone with a look, using the force of the air around them. He can remove the air from anywhere, causing you to suffocate. Whirlwinds, fires, tsunamis... all kinds of crazy shit. You don't realize how much air plays into things until you can control it. We do our best to keep Alec calm. When he loses control, he sometimes loses control of his powers. Like the rest of us, as he's gotten older, he's gotten more of a handle on it, but I feel a breakdown coming, and I have a feeling it's going to be a bad one.

Lenny and I are immortal, well, not entirely. We *can* die, but we heal a lot quicker than normal, making it awfully hard for us to die. Another thing we used to mess around with when we were younger. *Our lives.* We'd take turns stabbing each other, watching the wounds heal instantaneously in front of our eyes. Never leave a scar. We learned the hard way it doesn't work for Callan and Alec. They are *definitely* mortal. They have scars to show it. Gods, how dumb were we?

And this girl... Friday. I can't tell what she is, but she is something. Something fierce. I have this indescribable feeling that she's something important, not only to us but our entire community. I look into her eyes, and something is there. It's like I can see past the surface of her bright golden eyes to what's hidden beneath, only I can't make out what it is. I think she's unaware of what she is because her powers seem muffled. Almost like *they* are in hiding. Or maybe she knows what she is, and she is hiding them. Maybe she's hiding from someone? I need more time to decide how to go about this. I don't want to scare her away. Telling her any of this could scare her, whether she knows or not. If she is hiding, she may freak out, thinking she's been found. If she doesn't know, then she may think we're all crazy. I need to get to know her better. She seems open-minded, especially after that little situation last night. The memory of it makes my cock hard all over again. I contemplate taking care of it myself, but the thought of her doing it for me is more appealing.

I'd rather wait. Save it all for her.

This trip we go on each year is the only thing we have left with each other. We've drifted apart over the years, doing our own thing once we didn't fall into place naturally. Our relationship eventually became baggage none of us wanted to carry around. We became a nuisance to one another, instead of the support we should have been. The problem with us being apart is we *need* to be together. We bonded at a young age. When we're apart, something is missing. It's like an itch you can never scratch. Yet, we all tolerate it because it's easier to handle that than face the reality that we'll never be more.

It's true for all of us, but it's the hardest on Alec. He needs us the most, even though he'd die before admitting it. We function when we aren't together because that's life. You have to in order to survive. But knowing we could have so much more is what drives me crazy. Knowing we could *be* so much better, but we just aren't. When we are together like this, we feel better, our powers are stronger. Even if we fight and argue, it's like our damn souls are soothed just by being next to each other. The problem is, we don't know how to be together anymore. We fight, and we get sick of each other all too quickly. Usually, by the end of these trips, we want to tear each other's throats out.

Friday caught us at the beginning of our trip, which should help us. We've only had a few spats so far. Maybe this time won't get as bad as it usually does because she's here. Maybe this time will be different.

I flick away the cigarette that's between my fingers, blowing out the rest of the smoke from my lungs. I turn to go back inside, but I go into my room instead. I walk over to Friday, standing at the edge of the bed to watch her sleep. She doesn't know I was with her in her motel room back in Ellbrooke. She has no idea I'd been watching her from the moment I first saw her. Sure, I let her see me sometimes, needing to talk to her, to hear her voice, to stare into her eyes, but mostly, she didn't see a damn thing. I've learned something about watching her sleep brings me peace. Maybe because I've always struggled with sleep. Vampires don't need as much as others, but when I don't get any, it's a real problem. Something that happens more often than not.

I let out a sigh, shoving my hands into my pockets as I focus on her face. Her parted lips, soft skin... she's beautiful. Fucking gorgeous. This girl is going to be our savior. She is going to bring us all back together. I feel it in my soul. This woman, she's *it* for us. I just know it.

Chapter Thirteen

FRIDAY

"Rise and shine, baby cakes. Get up, we're going for breakfast."

I growl in response, burying my face in the pillow.

What time is it?

Why am I being woken up?

Just... why?

"Come on, sleepy head. I'm hungry." Lenny starts off in a sing-song voice that ends on a whine. I huff out a breath, not ready to get out of the soft, warm bed. I want to stay here forever, relishing this calm feeling.

The memories of last night come back to me and a rush of warmth fills my belly, it doesn't help with getting out of bed. In fact, it makes me want to pull Lenny into bed with me and ride him until *he* begs *me* to stop. My god, what is wrong with me? I barely know these guys and I keep thinking about them sexually.

I swipe the covers off me only to realize I'm completely naked. *Oops*. Lenny is standing at the foot of the bed, staring at me with his arms crossed and a smirk on his face. He's dressed adorably in fitted tan shorts and a red button-up. I can't see his shoes, but I bet dollars to donuts he has on the red Converse again. His shiny hair is tucked neatly behind his ears, loosely falling by his shoulders. I want to run my fingers through it... again. I watch as his bright blue eyes scan over my body and flash with want. It feels so good to be looked at like that.

Fuck it.

I wasn't modest last night, and I'm not going to start now. I crawl toward the end of the bed, biting my bottom lip and keeping eye contact with Lenny's gorgeous blue eyes. I get off the bed slowly, trying to be sexy about it. I'm not sure I succeed because pretending to be a stripper is not my thing. I have no rhythm—*at all*. When I see the look in Lenny's eyes, though, I know it worked. The hunger is back and burning hotter than it was only a moment ago. I saunter over to my bags and bend at the waist, digging through them trying to find something to wear. Lenny swears under his breath, but then I hear this awful choking sound that has me freezing.

I straighten and turn to see Callan in the conjoined doorway, standing there as red as a strawberry. I didn't even think it was possible for someone to turn that red. The image he just saw... holy shit. I look at Lenny with wide eyes and he bursts out laughing. He drops to his knees, covers his face and shakes with laughter. He then falls completely to the floor... still laughing. I shake my head, grab my clothes, using them to shield my nipples and vag, and scurry into the bathroom to get dressed. I bite my cheek to stop my own laughing, especially after seeing Callan scurry away. He's probably hiding under the bed like a scared animal; he may be there for a while. Poor guy.

I decide on high-waist red shorts with a white, loose-fitting crop top. Then I throw my hair up in an extra messy bun. I could put on make-up, but it's too early for that. I use the mouthwash I find on the sink and make a mental note to let the guys know I need to pick up a toothbrush. I slide on my flip-flops and walk out of the bathroom to find all four of the guys waiting for me. I don't think Alec is actually waiting for *me*, he's just waiting to leave.

Lenny sees me and he sucks his bottom lip between his teeth. I love this little back and forth game that's started between us. His flirting is obvious and exciting. This is going to be fun. Maddox makes eye contact, but quickly looks away without his expression changing. Callan's eyes are glued to his phone, his face still a light shade of pink, but I'm not convinced he's actually doing something. I'm pretty sure he's trying to avoid me.

"You guys ready?" I ask.

"Well, it's about damn time," Maddox grunts. "Let's go before we all die of starvation." I roll my eyes, snatch up my purse, and head toward the door.

"Oh, please, you guys are far from starving," I sass as I pass them.

"Hey, are you calling me fat?" Lenny whines as he follows me out the door. I ignore it.

We walk to the car and Maddox opens the door for me. I walk past him and open the door for the back seat.

"What do you think you're doing?" He looks at me with a disturbingly confused expression on his face.

"Sitting in the back. Is that a problem?" I look at Callan and wink at him. His complexion had gone back to its normal shade, but the wink brought it back to pink. Maddox notices the exchange, and he throws his head back and swears up at the sky. "What's the matter, big guy? Don't like not getting your way?" I pout my lip, giving his firm shoulder a squeeze before sliding into the backseat. I scoot to the middle; Alec gets in on my left and Lenny squishes in on my right. We all buckle up, my hand brushing Alec's as we both clip in our seatbelt at the same time. He quickly pulls his hand away and moves as close to the door as he can, leaving quite a bit of room between us like I've been diagnosed with the black plague.

"I'm not fucking diseased, you know." I scoff.

"Ignore him." The comment comes from Maddox, who is sitting in the driver's seat.

We drive just under ten minutes to a small diner. The building is full of windows and looks like it's covered in tin foil. I don't mind these small towns and their diners. Actually, I kind of love them. The food is comforting and always delicious. A nice change from the fast food I'm used to eating. Neither fuckwad nor I cooked often. Diner food has a sort of homemade feel to it, and I think that's what I love most.

Alec opens the door before the car comes to a complete stop, jumping out of the car as if it's on fire, ready to blow up at any second. The rest of us pile out, and Callan holds the diner door open for everyone. There is a sign placed by the door letting us know we can sit ourselves. The place isn't busy, and we have plenty of tables to choose from. Alec leads us to the back of the diner to a U-shaped booth, parking his ass right on the end.

"Move," Maddox tells Alec in a no-bullshit kind of tone. Alec stands without a word. Maddox glances at me with a smile. "Ladies first." I find myself clenching my thighs together. Why? Maddox's tone, that's why. The things he could make me do if he talked to me in that tone all the time.

I scoot in, Maddox sits to my left and Alec sits back down on the end. On my right is Lenny, with Callan on his. The waitress comes over, immediately handing out menus and asking what we would like to drink. We all order coffee and juice. I look over the menu, deciding I'm in the mood for pancakes. I haven't had good pancakes in a while.

When the waitress returns, she takes our food orders. Each of the guys orders two whole meals each. I know I shouldn't be, but for some reason, ordering only three pancakes makes me feel self-conscious. I'm the normal one here. I shouldn't be the one feeling some type of way.

"You guys hungry, or what?" I remark.

"Oh, this is nothing. You should see us when we are really, *really* hungry," Lenny states playfully, while adding way too much cream and sugar to his coffee. I study each of them, watching how they take their coffee. The way you drink coffee says a lot about your personality—it sounds silly, but it's something I've always believed. Alec drinks his black. Yeah, I could have told anyone that. Callan puts a normal amount of *milk* and sugar in his. Maddox makes his the same way I have mine: with cream only.

We chit chat back and forth about nothing in particular until we see two waitresses walking toward our table, each with a giant tray filled with food. They pass out the plates that take up the whole table and everyone starts eating right away. I'm the last to finish, and I'm not sure how that happened since I had the least amount of food. I don't question them. They're men, they should eat. No one seems to be in a rush to leave, so we sit back and let our stomachs settle while finishing our coffee.

"Tell me more about you guys. I told you my shit in the car, but you all haven't told me anything." I look at each of them, minus Alec, who is doing something on his phone. He must have a really good battery on that thing to never put it down.

"Not much to say," Maddox says, sipping his coffee.

"How do you all know each other?" I ask.

"We grew up together. We lived in the same neighborhood, went to the same schools. Our parents were not kind, so we understand the mom thing you mentioned. But we, at least, had each other. We did everything together," Callan answers, staring me down with his bright green eyes. Oh? So, he's looking at me again and his skin is a normal shade.

"I see. And what exactly is his deal?" I tip my head toward Alec.

"He hates everyone. Isn't that right, Alec?" Lenny teases in a voice people use to talk to babies. He's going to get punched. I can see it now.

Alec responds with a flip of his middle finger but doesn't pull his eyes from his phone.

"He loves us though, don't let his assholeness fool you," Lenny says.

"Assholeness?" I question, raising an eyebrow.

"Making up words is a hobby of mine," Lenny explains with an exaggerated wink that makes me laugh. He taps the side of his head. "Good imagination."

"Do you guys normally pick up girls during your annual men's road trip?" I ask the much-anticipated question. The thing I've been wondering from the beginning.

"This is actually the first," Callan answers, causing me to smile. I like that he's still talking to me after what he saw this morning.

"You guys married? Girlfriends... kids? What?"

"No." Maddox breathes out a haughty laugh. "Nothing like that." I narrow my eyes at him, feeling a little offended over his tone, like it was a ridiculous question. I didn't think it was.

"Do you have any siblings?" Callan pushes his glasses up his nose, folding his hands together, and placing them on the table in front of him.

"None that I know of, but I also don't know my father. So, it's a possibility," I say, shrugging and sipping the last bit of my cranberry juice. "You?"

"None of us have siblings," Callan answers quickly, almost like he doesn't want me to dig into that. Seems weird, but okay.

"Something we have in common." I tilt my head to the side, examining Callan. He looks nervous. Talking to me must really be tough for him.

"Indeed."

Our dark-haired waitress walks over and places the bill face down on the table. "No rush, whenever y'all are ready," she says, popping her gum.

"Let's go back to the motel and find something to do." Maddox slides toward the edge of the booth and we all follow his lead. He stops at the counter to pay the bill while the rest of us walk out the door and get into the Jeep. I sit in the back again, between Lenny and Alec. Not sure what Alec's problem is, but I'm going to break past it. I'm very likable... as long as I *want* you to like me. He can't ignore me forever. It's impossible. I don't care how much of an asshole he *thinks* he is, he's no match for Friday McKay.

CHAPTER FOURTEEN

LENNY

The more time I spend with Friday, the more I think Maddox is right. I trust him more than anyone else in this world. I would follow him blindly. Yeah, he'd probably fuck with me for a bit, but he would never intentionally steer me in the wrong direction. I never question his intentions. But when it comes to Friday, I'm starting to realize it for myself. I think once I let the others know what I'm feeling, Callan will come around. As for Alec? He'll either have to suck it up and stick around or leave. Those are the only options. I have no idea what would happen to us if he left. We'd be incomplete again, unless he officially rejected us and cut all ties.

Maddox's idea of finding something to do was lounging around and watching TV. We'd have been better off at the diner—at least there we had food. I'm hungry, again. As usual. I glance around the room wondering if anyone else wants food too. Friday is sitting beside me, watching whatever is playing on the TV. Alec is taking up the other bed, on his phone, which is what he's been doing this entire trip. Maddox and Callan are both in desk chairs not too far from me. Everyone is engrossed in what they're doing. I doubt anyone is hungry again. It's been less than two hours since we ate, but man, I really could use more food.

Aside from being hungry, I'm itching to use my magic. Something tells me it has to do with Friday. Usually it's manageable, but ever since last night, it's been different. I half expect to look down and see my skin glowing because that's exactly how it feels. I'm going to have to sneak out at some point to let some of it out. Maybe I can get Mad to come with me and I can talk to him then. I pick up my phone to send him a text. Our powers are cool, but if we could talk to each other telepathically, that would be fucking awesome.

Me: We gotta go out when she goes to sleep.

Maddox: Need more already?

Me: Not for that, jerkoff. It's something else.

Maddox: Fine.

The phone in my hand reminds me...

"Has your ex contacted you lately?" My question causes Maddox and Callan to turn their gazes to me and Friday. I like that Callan is showing interest in her. I was worried because I know how he can be. Him and females don't mix. He's coming out of his shell a bit, which is something he never does. I like it. I like seeing him talking to a girl. To *our* girl.

"Not since the last time I told you guys. I think he's given up, or just busy getting fucked again, who knows," Friday says. Her gaze is still on the TV, and she seems really into whatever it is they're all watching. I can't remember what it is because

I haven't been paying attention, and watching it now, nothing looks familiar.

"Does it bother you?" Callan asks. His tone is soft. It's blowing my mind the way he's acting with her. I've never seen him open up so much to someone outside of our group before.

Friday pulls her attention from the movie and looks at Callan thoughtfully. Then she shrugs and says, "Not really, to be honest. At first, I was mad... furious, but I wasn't ever upset. We didn't belong together. We weren't happy and we were bound to break up anyway. It wasn't... right. You know how some things just don't *feel* right?"

"Or the times when they do?" My eyes widen at the sound of Maddox's voice. Bold of him to make a comment like that, though I shouldn't be surprised. He's never been one to keep his mouth shut. I don't think she'll get what he's talking about, but we do.

It gets quiet then, and it feels weird as hell. "Who's hungry? Can we order some food?" I speak the words quickly and get to my feet. "Callan, you hungry? Maddox?" They both shake their heads.

"Are you ever not fucking hungry?" Alec grunts, tossing his phone onto the bed and resting his back as he closes his eyes.

Friday gasps and her hand goes to her mouth as she points at Alec. I glance from her to him, trying to figure out what the hell is going on. Did I miss something?

"It speaks!" she squeaks. I bark out a laugh, and I swear I saw the corner of his mouth twitch. Hard to believe, but I know what I saw. She giggles and then drops her hand, turning to me. "I could eat. Come on, Lenny, let's go find some food." Friday stands up, slipping her flip-flops on and starts toward the door.

"Mad? Keys, please." I smile big at him. I know full well he doesn't like anyone driving his Jeep. I've only driven it a handful of times and he'd kill me, no exaggeration, if I ever did anything to it. That Jeep is his baby.

He takes the keys off the bureau and holds them over my open palm. "Crash the car, and you die."

See. That car is worth more than my life. I roll my eyes.

"Yeah, sure." I snatch the keys from his hand as he tries to pull them away. "Too slow, ya old fart." Friday bursts out laughing, and we take off toward the car as Maddox sputters off something I can't make out.

"Do you really think he's old? How old are *you*?" Friday asks as she buckles her seatbelt. I buckle my own and start the car before answering.

"Twenty-five, and no. He just gets so bent out of shape when I fuck with him. Getting him riled up is my lifelong goal." I back out of the spot carefully, knowing if I crash this thing, I better do it far away from Maddox.

Sometimes, I think I was put on this earth to teach people patience, especially Maddox. I know I can be a lot to handle. I'm hyper and full of energy most of the day. I'm not always easy to deal with for that reason, but I'm so lovable, people can't help but want to be with me. And *that* is how they learn patience. Maddox has taught me so much over the years, but I know the same is true the other way around.

"So, the thing with you and Maddox..." Her voice is careful, as if she doesn't know if she should be asking this. "Is he always like that? You know, an asshole?"

"When you get to know Maddox, you learn he isn't an asshole, he just gives you the hard truths you don't want to hear in a not so nice way. He doesn't sugar coat things."

"And you're okay with that?"

I shrug as I come to a red light and stop. This thing with Maddox is complicated and that's why we don't talk about it.

We just let it be whatever it is. We've never had a reason to talk about it before, but that may change.

"Maddox is an acquired taste. He's done so much for me in my life. I love him so damn much and I would do anything for him. I'm fine with whatever it is that goes on with us."

That's not the most direct answer, but I can't get into too much detail about it without telling her *everything*.

She nods, then turns to me with a smirk that I catch from my peripheral. "Can I ask you something more personal?"

I grin. "Go for it."

"Do you guys ever switch?"

I raise a brow, turning to her, the grin still planted on my face. "Nah," I say, turning back toward the road. "It's not really his thing, and before you ask, *yes*, I am okay with it."

She smiles again, then turns back in her seat to face the front. It's quiet for a stretch before Friday speaks again. "Where are we going?"

"I saw a pizza place around here somewhere when we drove in, I just have to remember where it was." She makes the most delicious sound with her mouth at the mention of pizza, and I'm tempted to pull over right now and show her that I *can* do the fucking... if I want.

"Let's find a liquor store. I want to get drunk," she suggests as she presses the button to put the radio on. Classic music blares through the speakers and she lowers it to a volume we can talk over.

Pizza and alcohol? This is a woman after my own heart.

"You got it, sweet cheeks." Friday laughs at my nickname and playfully swats at my arm. She's so easy to get along with and talk to. It feels like I've known her forever.

The pizza place isn't far, and it doesn't take me long to find it. I may have used a silent spell to help me, but no one needs to know about that. I'm still itching to use my magic, that tiny bit

I allowed myself did nothing to scratch it. I was going to use my GPS, but we both realized we forgot our phones since we ran out of the room so quickly, afraid of being mauled by the Big Bad Wolf. The parking lot for the pizzeria only has a few cars in it, and it's side by side with a gas station convenience store that has a large sign in the window saying they sell liquor.

Hell. Yes.

I raise an eyebrow. "I'll get the pizza; you get the liquor?"

"Got it." We get out of the car and head in opposite directions.

The bell above the door dings as I walk inside, and the smell of fresh baked bread washes over me, making my mouth water. The guys said they weren't hungry, but I know better than that. If I go back there without enough food for all of them, they'll bitch. Especially if we start drinking. I get to the counter and order six large pizzas. I can, and plan to, eat one by myself. Then we'll have extras for later too. Callan ordered the pizza last night, and I told him three wasn't enough. Yeah, we were all satisfied, but I could have had more if there had been some.

The tall skinny guy behind the counter lets me know it'll be a bit because they're made to order. He doesn't seem happy to have someone ordering so much food if the scowl on his face says anything. I pay him, then head outside, figuring I'll go help Friday, but as soon as I round the corner, I see her walking out of the store carrying two large paper brown bags.

This girl is ready to party.

Fuck, yes.

I take both bags from her even though she tries arguing with me about it. She opens the back door on the driver's side and puts the bags on the floor.

"Pizza will be a little while. What did you get?"

"All sorts of stuff. I wasn't sure what you all like to drink."

"Let's wait in the car, the people in there don't seem very friendly," I say, pointing toward the pizza place. She chuckles and gets into the car.

"What's your story, Lenny?" she asks, turning to me. I put the key back in the ignition to turn the car on so the air conditioner will keep it cool.

"My story? It's not a good one." I run a hand through my hair tucking the stray strands behind my ear. "All of us grew up together in the same neighborhood. Our parents were all shitty in their own way. Mine, though? It's hard to say she was the worst. What she did was messed up, but I don't think anything can beat what Alec's mom did. That's his story to tell, though, so I won't get into it." I turn to face Friday, lifting my knee up onto the seat. The sun shining through the window causes the red in her hair to glimmer and her golden eyes to shine bright. Gods, this girl is beautiful. "Anyway, it doesn't matter who was worse or not. They were all awful, but basically, my mother abandoned me when I was only eight."

"Oh, that's—"

"But she didn't just leave me with like family or something. She took off and left me in our house alone. I don't know if she wanted me to die or hoped someone would find me. Luckily, I already knew the guys at that point. Maddox did find me and took care of me. We never told anyone she left. I don't know where she is right now. Probably dead."

"What about school... bills? How did you stay in the house alone?"

"Maddox was working at the time. He made sure the bills were paid. There weren't many since the house was paid for. He made sure I was up every day for school. He walked me there and back. It's not like we had anyone to tell. None of the other guys' parents would have cared, and if we told someone at the school or the police, they would have taken me, and Maddox couldn't have me away from them because of the—" Shit, shit, shit. I almost said too much.

Friday gives me a confused look.

"Ya know, just because... *us.*" *Good save, Lenny.* "Because we'd known each other for so long, we were family. If I got put into the system, I'd probably never see them again. Was it the right thing to do? Probably not, but he did a great job. I owe him my life. I stayed at his place most of the time. His mom didn't know the difference."

All of this stuff with my mother happened around the time he realized he wasn't human. He'd done so much research and knew right away the four of us were mates. Maddox is so smart and so quick on his feet. I really do owe him everything.

"Is that how you guys... ya know?" She brushes her hair off her shoulder, her bright eyes on mine.

"Started fucking?" I huff out a laugh. "No, that hasn't been going on for *that* long. Few years now, and not very often." I chuckle again as I think about it. It's only been a short amount of time since we started having sex, but there is so much involved with me and Maddox that it's hard to pinpoint when and where the feelings changed and became more. I love Callan and I love Alec, but not the way I love Maddox.

"Have you two been with other guys?"

"As far as I know, he hasn't. I messed around with a few guys in high school. It's not really a gender thing for me, I just like having fun. It's hard to explain," I say, running my hand through my hair again. "It's never been like how it is with Maddox, though."

"Tell me about the first time." She licks her bottom lip before sucking it between her teeth. My dick stirs at the thought of her getting off on Maddox and I being together.

I smirk, then recall the first time Maddox and I were together. "We live in the same city, not far from one another. The other guys live further away, but Maddox and I spend a lot of time together. We were hanging out one night, drinking, and it just happened."

She takes a few strands of her hair twirling them around her finger—possibly an innocent gesture, but right now, it's turning me on, and I have no idea why. My cock starts to grow harder.

"That's it?" She blinks innocently.

This girl...

She wants details? I can give her details.

"We were at his house, sitting on the couch watching hockey or something. I can't exactly remember, but it was definitely a sport. We were talking about the guys and the upcoming trip, just hanging out and drinking. It was like every other time we hang out, but this time... Maddox just kissed me. Out of nowhere, he just leaned over and kissed me. At first, it freaked me out. I didn't kiss him back, not right away. It took a few seconds for me to realize I liked it. Once I felt how hard my dick was, I went with it. Of course he took full control of the situation, which I fucking loved."

"More." Her hands move to her thighs, and she slowly slides them up and between her legs, leaving them there to rest. My eyes stay there for a moment, before bringing them back up to meet hers.

"We made out for a while. Maddox was on top of me, grinding his cock against mine until neither of us could take it any longer. He unbuttoned my pants and took my cock in his hand. Fuck, I swear I almost came right then and there. The feeling of his hand on me? Gods, it was so hot." I blow out a breath and shake my head as I get lost in the memory for a moment. "He jerked me off, slowly, like he was trying to figure it out. I know he'd never done anything like that before that made it almost unbearably sexy. After a bit, he flipped me over, started to fumble with his jeans..." I pause, taking in the way she's sitting, how her legs have spread, and her cheeks are tinged pink.

Her hand slides up her thighs, closer to her pussy that I could really use another taste of right now. I lick my lips, unable to pull my eyes away. Her fingers reach her center, and she rubs herself through her shorts, her hips moving off the seat in rhythm with her hand... so fucking slow.

My cock is so damn hard it hurts.

All I can do is watch as she keeps it up, keeps sliding her fingers up and down over her pussy. There is no way she'll get off like that... right? She needs more. Gods, I want to give her more. Soft moans fill the car and I'm two seconds away from taking my cock out and putting it in her mouth. I'm reaching for the button when there's a loud knock on my window. I swear we both jump through the roof, and I nearly shit my pants.

"Hey! You ordered six pizzas?" someone shouts.

I turn toward the window and give a thumbs up, my heart pounding in my damn chest. The look on Friday's face when I turn back to her has me losing it. I try to hold back the laugh but there's no stopping it. She joins me, the car filled with laughter until there's tears falling down our faces. My vision is blurry as we make it into the pizza shop. I'm still cracking up as I pull out my wallet and almost drop the pizzas on the way back to the car.

Once we're back in the car, the whole mood changes and I'm swept back into the memory of her touching herself and my cock is hard all over again.

The car is quiet as I pull out of the lot and head back toward the motel. We're on a long stretch of road surrounded by nothing but trees when my dick starts to throb, reminding me how badly I want to fuck her. My hands tighten on the steering wheel, and I decide I don't want to wait for this. I pull over, skidding to a stop in the dirt on the side of the road. It's broad daylight, but I don't care. I get out of the car, storm around to her side, and yank open the door. I reach around her to unclick the seatbelt before pulling her out by her arms. The look on her face is priceless: part shock, part fear, but one hundred percent excitement. I kiss her hard, my tongue diving into her mouth to stroke hers. I shift us, pressing her back against the car and grinding against her, showing her what she's done to me. The slight bit of pressure against my dick has me groaning and wanting more. I blindly reach to the handle to the back door and pull it open as I move us again, shoving her toward the back seat.

"Get in and bend over," I whisper against her lips.

She climbs in and I climb in right after her, shutting the door behind us. I undo my pants as she settles into the seat on her knees, facing the back. I glance down at her ass, her perfectly round, full ass that I'd love nothing more than to bury my tongue and dick in. One day, but not today. Once I'm free, I slide my fingers into the waistband of her shorts and tug them down. I groan as I take in the view, running my fingers gently over the curve of her ass. I position myself behind her, gripping the seat for leverage. I notch the head of my dick at her swollen, sopping wet pussy. A shiver runs through my body as the heat radiates from her, as her pussy clenches, wanting to suck me in. I lean forward and kiss her neck, then another down her spine. She arches into me, a sharp breath releasing from her.

"Lenny..." she pleads, a half moan, half whine.

"I got you," I tell her as I grip her hip, and then slide into her so slowly. Fuck, she feels better than I expected her too. She's tight, and wet, and oh so fucking warm. She gasps as I push my cock deeper, taking me all in. I settle inside her for a moment, taking a second to breathe and enjoy how fucking good she feels. But then she's whimpering my name and pushing her ass against me. I chuckle.

"I said I got you." I kiss her shoulder this time, then pull out and slam into her. She throws her head back, her hair whipping around her as she cries out this delicious sound that has me wanting to do everything in my power to hear it again.

I groan as I fuck her, my hips slapping against her ass with each thrust.

"Play with your pussy," I tell her. "I need to feel you come on my cock."

She does as she's told, sliding her hand between her legs. Her pussy flutters around me, and I know I won't be lasting long. Especially when she reaches down and cups my balls, massaging them with her soft fingers. There's nothing else but us right now, just her and I inside this car. If someone drove by, I couldn't tell you. If we're seen, too fucking bad. I slam into her harder when I feel the tell-tale sign of an orgasm.

"Fuck," I rasp out just as she releases my balls and goes back to playing with her clit.

"Lenny, I'm gonna—fuck!" She comes with a loud cry, her body convulsing under the weight of mine, a few more pumps and I'm a goner. Her orgasm takes my own from me and I empty inside of her. Pulse after pulse after fucking pulse, it's never ending. I'm blinded by the euphoria of a full-body orgasm, and it takes me a minute to even remember where we are. I stay inside her for a few moments, resting my head on her back and just trying to catch my breath.

She starts to shake beneath me, and I jerk back, slipping out of her and have to fight to not watch my cum drip from her because damn that's so fucking sexy, but... Is she crying?

"Are you okay?" I ask as I press my hand to her shoulder. The sound that comes out of her has me breathing a sigh of relief and a chuckle to leave me. She isn't crying; she's laughing. Thank fuck.

I glance down at the seat below her. Maddox is going to fucking kill me for getting cum on his seat.

"God, Lenny, that was fucking awesome," she shouts through laughing.

I chuckle again, then fall to the seat beside her, squished between her warm body and the warm pizza boxes. Probably best we don't tell the guys about this, they may not want to eat the pizza. Though, maybe that's a reason to tell them about it? I'll have it all to myself.

I slide my arm around Friday's waist and tug her to my lap. She rests her head on my shoulder and sighs, nuzzling into me. I kiss her temple, then run my fingers through her hair. I don't want to move, don't want to let this girl go. I can't and I won't. The guys better get on board with this, and fast, because there is no way this girl is leaving me. I won't let her.

As I drive back to the motel, the thought of how stupid that was won't leave my mind. I just fucked this girl without a condom. What if she isn't on birth control? This is why I didn't fuck her last night; I knew we didn't have any condoms. Why would we? That's not what this trip is about. I should probably stop and pick some up. I'm not really worried about the STD thing; it's different for paranormals and unlikely I'd catch anything. Or, if I did, whatever it is, is curable.

I swallow hard before opening my mouth and trying to speak. "Do you, uh... have you..."

"Birth control?" Her tone is playful, and I can tell she's trying not to laugh at me. I nod, my hands tightening around the steering wheel, worried about what she's going to say. I'm not ready to be a dad. Not even close. "Yeah, Lenny, we're good. I'm not *that* stupid." She pats my chest and then turns toward the window. I sneak a glance at her, and my heart warms over the bright smile on her face.

Yeah, I'm definitely not letting this girl go.

Chapter Fifteen

Maddox

Lenny and Friday get back close to two hours after leaving. No way in fuck it took that long to get pizza. You could drive around this town ten times and still be back in under an hour, never mind two. *They fucked.* I know it. I can feel it. And I'm pissed about it. We'd agreed not to move further with any of this, not until we knew what was going on. Leave it to Lenny to ignore anything I say, always having to push my god damn buttons.

Lenny can be a little shit, but he is smart. At least, he can be when he takes the time to think before acting, which isn't always the case. He may have fucked up by fucking her, but he did good by getting as many pizzas as he did. We'll still have plenty for dinner, so we shouldn't have to go out again tonight. We can spend the rest of the day lounging inside and doing nothing. Well, not nothing, because apparently, Friday is ready to party.

"Who's getting drunk with me?" she asks, holding up a bottle of vodka.

"Oh, me, me, me!" Lenny bounces up and down on his knees, waving his hands in the air. His childish antics make Friday laugh. That *fucker*. I hate how easily they're getting along, how quickly they've formed a relationship already.

I watch as they chat and laugh, Friday's smile a mile wide, and Lenny's eyes full of adoration. I grit my teeth as I stare them down. They definitely fucked.

"Is that really a good idea, *Leonard*?" I ask, though I'm pretty sure they've moved on to another conversation by now.

"Don't fucking call me that, Maddox," he growls at me.

He hates when anyone calls him that because it's what his mother called him, but it's the only way I know to get his full attention, for him to know I'm not fucking playing around. Lenny is hard to control when he's drinking and tends to be a little too free with his magic. We can't have that shit happening tonight.

"We need to talk." I force the words out and don't wait for an answer. I walk straight to the door, ignoring the dirty look Friday is shooting my way. She probably thinks I'm the big asshole who is going to ruin her buzz and fuck up their night. Well, too fucking bad. Someone's gotta keep shit in line.

I step outside, and allow the door to close behind me, I walk around the building lighting up a smoke on the way, knowing Lenny will be here any minute. I'm almost finished with my cigarette when he finally makes his way outside.

He stands in front of me with his long arms crossed over his chest, a frown on his boyish face. "The fuck, Mad?"

"Do you really think it's a good idea to get drunk around Friday? You know how you get." I take the last drag from my cigarette and then flick it away. I pull another from the pack and put it between my lips before lighting it up.

"I don't think that's any of your fucking business, Maddox." He raises his hand, and a small neon yellow ball forms a few inches above his palm. He tosses it to his other hand, then back. It gets bigger the more he throws it until it's the size of a grapefruit. It illuminates the area around us, and gives off a slight buzzing sound, like a livewire. I know he's been itching to use his magic, and though paranormals aren't unheard of, I'd rather Friday not know that's what we are yet. I just have a bad feeling about it.

I step closer to him and look up. Lenny's got a few good inches on me but is a good fifty pounds lighter. He doesn't carry muscle the way I do, though it's because he doesn't want to. He's lazy as hell, and I'm surprised he doesn't weigh four hundred pounds because of it. Especially with the trash he eats.

I point my finger at him. "It is my business, *Leonard*, and you know it."

"Stop calling me that!" he growls out, dropping his energy ball that falls to the ground and splits into a thousand little marble-sized balls before disappearing. He clenches his hands at his sides and steps even closer, glaring down at me. Well, at least I have his attention.

"What did you need to talk to me about, anyway?" I step away and lean against the brick wall, sure he gets my point. We need to find out more about Friday before she starts to learn our secrets. Even if I am certain she is our mate, I can't guarantee she is going to be okay with it and stick around like this is the best opportunity to come her way.

"Alec," Lenny says simply.

"He's a dick, what about him?"

Lenny paces back and forth, tugging out the hair tie and letting his hair fall around his shoulders. He gathers it all together before pulling it to the back of his head and tying it in another somehow perfectly messy bun. I'll never understand how he does that.

"I think you're right about Friday, but what if Alec leaves? What do we do then? He needs a fucking intervention or something. I don't know how to get through to him, what to do, but I'm worried. Friday, she's it. I know it." He stops in front of me, his mouth opening and closing a few times like he has more to say but can't get it out. He goes back to pacing, shaking his head and mumbling to himself.

"Lenny," I call but he ignores me and keeps pacing. "*Lenny!*" I shout, and he finally stops and looks at me, his bright eyes dark with worry. "Don't worry about Alec. I'll take care of him. He's not leaving, he's not going anywhere, we will be fine."

"But, Mad, it's been like—"

"I get it, I really do, but it's not your problem. I will handle it." I step toward him. "I promise you, it'll be fine. Just stop worrying about it. You and Friday seem to be getting on great, so do me a favor. We need to know if she knows about any of this. It's vital to all of this and I haven't figured out how to go about it without freaking her out." I flash him a smile. "You're better at the nice stuff than me. Find out how much she knows, and I'll do the rest, okay?" He nods.

"Yeah, okay. I can do that."

"How do you think she's going to take all this?"

"She's a badass, Mad." He smirks, scratching the back of his neck. "Honestly, I think she will be fine. She'll probably be excited."

I finish my cigarette and toss it to the ground. "Good to know."

"Am I good?" he questions. One thing Lenny almost always has is respect. I taught him you only get respect when you give it, but you should always give it as a default.

"You're good," I tell him. With another nod, he moves toward the door, but stops short, whirling around toward me. What the hell does he need now?

"Oh, by the way... I fucked her in the Jeep." He grins and scurries inside.

"Fucker," I grumble.

I rest my head against the cold brick of the building, a smile creeping across my face. For the first time in a long time, I feel like we are all going to be okay.

Chapter Sixteen

CALLAN

Friday is drunk, completely obliterated. White girl wasted kind of drunk, as I've heard some people say. I'm not into the popular slang, but it really encompasses what she is right now. It is a bit much. She's been dancing around in her underwear for the last half hour, around me and even *on* me. I wish she would stop. Don't get me wrong, I can appreciate a woman, especially one with a body like hers. She's curvy in all the right places. She smells delicious, especially her long wavy hair that is flopping around in my face, but I am quite uncomfortable. I'll admit it's not a hard thing to accomplish, many things make me uncomfortable, but that's not the point.

It doesn't help that the moment she came into our room in her underwear, my dick has been hard. It's not easy to hide, and if anyone notices, I will never live it down. Lucky for me, I think *she's* too drunk to notice, and the guys are paying more attention to her than anything else.

I keep looking to Lenny for help, who is sitting on one of the beds. His eyes are glued to Friday, and he has a permanent smile on his face. This kind of situation is his specialty, it's what he thrives in, but do you think he'd help me? Of course not. He keeps laughing at me, even though I'm staring at him wide-eyed, silently pleading for help. Every now and then, he joins in with her, making things worse. Just a few minutes ago, he was dancing on me too. I'm not a violent person, but I wanted to punch him.

Maddox is hiding out in the corner, doing something on his phone. He glances up every now and then with a fire in his eyes I have never seen before. I can't tell if it's anger or something else, but I think it's something else. I can't imagine what he would be angry about. It's no secret Maddox enjoys women...

He did seem a little more grumpy than usual when he came back inside from talking with Lenny. No clue what that's about, but I stopped trying to figure them two out long ago. The one thing in life I just can't figure out is people. Such a shame, because they're so interesting.

Alec is lying on the bed furthest away from the *party* with his back to us. He could be sleeping, but I doubt it. I keep silently praying Friday won't make her way over there and poke the bear. That is not something I want to deal with tonight... or ever. I cannot imagine the repercussions of that situation. It may be the last time we see him.

I trust Maddox, I always have. He's taken on a leadership role and has always done his best to keep us going. Regardless of how tough he acts on the outside, I know deep down he cares about us and the mate relationships. He has hope, he holds onto it and uses it to keep us all going. He's the reason we're all here right now, he's the one who pushes us to keep doing this, and I have to be grateful for that. Especially because I think he's right about Friday.

Chapter Seventeen

FRIDAY

I wake up next to a sleeping, very sexy, and very *naked* Maddox. I pray to the universe we did not have sex last night. And not because I don't want to, because it's been a thought in my mind since I first saw him, but because I don't remember it and that would be the disappointment of the century. If Maddox and I fucked, I'd need to remember it so I could relive it over and over again in my mind. I sit up, realizing right away I have clothes on—a T-shirt and underwear. Okay, that's a good sign. My gaze goes back to Maddox, who's lying on his stomach, the muscles in his back are a damn art form. Especially with all of the tattoos covering it. I get a better look at them now that I'm this close. The intricate designs and details are amazing, especially with no color. There are words, faces, flowers, skulls, roses, thorns... it's like a whole story being told, but one I don't know. It takes everything in me to not reach over and run my fingers across his very tempting skin.

Yeah, I want to fuck him bad... really bad. But I also need to keep my pride intact. It's one of the only things I have. I can't throw myself at guys like him. Lenny is a different story. He's Lenny, and it just felt... right and normal. With Maddox, he's too cocky for me to give it up so easily; it'll go straight to his head. So no, as tempting as he is, he needs to work for it, so I can keep him in check. I look over to the other bed and notice it's empty. I expected Lenny to be asleep there, considering Maddox is in bed with me, but the sheets aren't even messed up. The adjoining door is opened only slightly, a dim light flickering from the other room.

I throw the blankets off me and get out of bed carefully, not wanting to wake the beast. If he touches me, I'll cave. I pull the handle to open the door and pop my head inside. Callan and Lenny are lying in one bed, both awake. Alec is in the other, sleeping. Both bears are hibernating, good.

"Friday!" Lenny squeaks.

"Shhh, you're going to wake him," Callan whispers, slapping Lenny on the arm and motioning toward Alec with the other. "I barely got any sleep. I don't want to deal with him right now."

My eyebrows go up in question as I glance at the clock. It's only about nine in the morning.

"Long story. Come here." Lenny taps the space on the bed between him and Callan. I waste no time squishing myself in between the two of them. This is something I could get used to—being squished between two guys. *Wow, Friday... what has happened to you?*

I'm just enjoying life, I guess.

The room is chilly, the air conditioner must be on high, but the warmth from the two guys I'm between is enough to make me comfortable, even though I'm only in a pair of panties and a

T-shirt. Callan shifts toward the edge of the bed, moving away from me.

"Come on, Cal, knock it off. She doesn't bite," Lenny says with a roll of his eyes.

I waggle my eyebrows at Lenny. "And how do you know that?"

"Good point." Lenny's gaze flicks to Callan. "Cal, I'll make sure she doesn't bite *you*. If she wants to bite someone, she can bite me." He looks back to me and snaps his teeth.

"Don't tempt me." I keep a playful tone, but really, I feel the wetness starting between my thighs. Lenny is fun, so much fun. And the sex was so good. Maybe that's because it's been a while, and douchebag was always just mediocre, but the chemistry with Lenny and I is so good, it made the sex great. He was so in tune with my body, touching me in all the right places, making everything good for me. And it wasn't weird afterward.

"Maybe I want to?" he teases.

I open my mouth to respond with something that very well could have us getting naked again, but Callan speaks first.

"Are you guys done? I'm trying to watch this movie." Callan gestures to the TV. He doesn't look like he's watching it. It's more like he's forcing himself to look at the television and not at me. His hand is resting on his belly, his shirt pulled up the tiniest bit, allowing me to see his skin and the light brown hair trailing beneath his pants. He's dressed for the day already, once again filling in a pair of jeans so nicely. I don't think he realizes how hot he is.

"I'm never done. You should know that by now, Cal."

"Unfortunately." His eyes shift to me, looking down at my bare legs then back to my eyes. "Don't you have pants?" He pushes his glasses up on the bridge of his nose, all businesslike.

"I'm sure she does, but I like her without them." Lenny hooks his hand around my thigh and pulls me closer to him, leaving his hand to rest on my thigh. "If you don't like it, don't look."

"Both of you need to shut the fuck up before I go over there and make you. Bad enough you kept me up all night with this bullshit," a growling voice sounds from across the room.

"Good job, *Cal.* You woke the asshole," Lenny whispers loudly. I slap my hand over my mouth to stop the laughing, but it doesn't really help. Callan is beet red again, only this time I think it's out of anger. He shakes his head and focuses back on the TV.

CHAPTER EIGHTEEN

ALEC

Those assholes kept me awake most of the night talking about Friday, the girl who is supposed to save us. And now, they still can't shut up and let me get some sleep. I have half a mind to go into the room with Maddox and lock the door behind me. Fuck, I have half a mind to leave all together and not come back. *The girl who is going to save us*? Do they really believe that shit? No one on this planet is capable of saving us... of saving me. I'm too far gone. I've accepted it and so should they. I've tried getting over what happened, there's no point. You can't just get over something like that, especially when the memories haunt me day and night, awake and sleeping. Nothing stops them from coming. Nothing.

I realize I am never going to get to sleep with Lenny's big mouth and Friday's annoying as fuck laugh, so I roll out of bed and plant my feet on the ground. Lenny makes a shushing sound as I walk by, and honestly? I like that they avoid me. I know it's a big joke to Lenny, but it still keeps them off my back and that's all I care about. I *want* to be left alone. I rub the sleep from my eyes as I move toward my bags. I dig through them and grab a change of clothes and head into the bathroom, trying to hide the fact my dick is rock hard. All thanks to the talk about Friday in her underwear *and* the image I caught of her laying between Lenny and Callan in said underwear. I fucking hate the way my body is reacting to her.

When she was dancing around the room last night, it took everything in me not to give her the attention I wanted to. I don't want to talk to her, and I don't want her to look at me. I just want to fuck her. Raw and savage. The dirtiest definition of the word. *Fuck.* And I have no fucking idea why I can't get the thought out of my head, but all it's doing is infuriating me. Twice last night I had to go to the bathroom to jerk off. *Twice.* In one night. I can't remember the last time I wanted to jerk off at all, never mind twice. Closing the door to the bathroom, I rest my head against it, completely defeated. My cock aches and I hate life and everything this fucked up universe has handed me.

I didn't do anything to deserve this shit. I deserve nothing that's happened to me over the years, and that's what pisses me off the most.

I turn the shower on and step in without waiting for it to get hot. Maybe the cold water will make my dick go back to normal.

I wash my body with the soap I brought with me, using my special shampoo for my beard. I'm totally distracted by my throbbing cock, and I end up washing up twice. There's no use trying to will it away, it just doesn't work that way. The only way to make it go away is to give in. I'm angry, so fucking angry. I don't want to jerk off thinking about this girl, don't want to cum with her name on my lips. Yet, that's exactly what the fuck I do. The worst part is? It takes no time at all. Minutes, even. Fucking pathetic.

The guilt hits when I'm done, feeling like a complete idiot for not being able to control a sexual craving. What the fuck is wrong with me?

I shut the water off and get out. I dry off and get dressed as quickly as I can before leaving the bathroom and getting my boots on. Then I head out the door because I need some fucking air.

Air that isn't tainted with her sweet fucking smell.

CHAPTER NINETEEN

FRIDAY

Alec stomps out of the room leaving a masculine, citrus scent in his wake. I would not object to being surrounded by that scent more often. What could have pissed him off in the shower, though? Is he really just that angry at the world? Something about that thought has me wanting to go after him. Maybe I should try talking to him, try to help him. He's made it clear he wants nothing to do with me, but everyone needs to know they have someone who cares about them. Another part of me, though, is saying *fuck him*. I'd much rather stay here in bed with the two hot guys that aren't dicks to me. I'm literally in a man sandwich right now. This is me, living my best life, and I'd be an idiot to give it up for someone who's been nothing but rude to me.

I turn my attention to Callan, my fantasies going wild.

"Have you ever been fucked before?" The words leave my mouth before I think better of them, but they're out now... nothing I can do about it.

Callan chokes, on what? I don't know. He didn't have anything in his mouth, but he pats his chest and tries to catch his breath the same time Lenny gasps and then barks out a laugh. It wasn't meant to be a joke, but whatever.

"Uhm, yeah? Obviously," Callan responds in a raspy voice, trying to get a hold on his coughing fit. He rubs his throat and tugs at his shirt, like it's too tight.

"Is that a question or are you sure?" I narrow my eyes at him. He doesn't seem confident in his answer. I think he's lying.

He shifts on the bed, sitting up a little straighter and keeping his gaze on the TV and clears his throat before saying, "Of course, I'm sure."

"And I thought I didn't have a filter," Lenny mumbles.

I look at him, give him a saucy wink and then roll over to face Callan. I scoot closer, so close I can feel the heat radiating from him, and I can smell whatever it is he puts in his hair. It smells good, expensive, fresh. I place my hand on his lower belly, the muscles there tense, and then the rest of his body does too. He isn't even breathing, but I sure can feel his heart thundering in his chest. I push up on my free elbow and move close to his ear and whisper, "Because if you're not sure..."

Callan chokes again and scrambles off the bed and out of my touch. He looks everywhere but at me, takes a step this way and then that way as if he doesn't know where to go. He finally decides to go into the bathroom, shutting the door harshly behind him. I roll onto my back and find Lenny staring at me with a raised brow and an impressed look on his face.

I shrug and smirk. "It's a gift."

It's been over an hour and Alec isn't back. I can't figure out why that worries me, why I care that he's gone.

"Have you guys heard from Alec?" All three guys answer in unison, giving me different variations of no.

Maddox strolled in here after Callan closed himself in the bathroom and gladly took his spot on the bed. When Callan came back into the room, he looked both disappointed and relieved. He then made himself comfortable on Alec's bed.

"You're not worried about him?" I question when they don't seem to care that he's just gone.

"I'm more worried for anyone he may run into. How pissed was he when he left?" Maddox stares at the TV, sitting against the headboard, wearing nothing but those gray sweatpants. I may have stolen a look or two... or three, to his, *ya know*. Actually, that's a lie. My eyes have looked over every inch of his body multiple times and I feel his proximity is affecting me more than it's affecting him. I hate it, but gods, do I love it at the same time. He's just so damn sexy. The wide chest, the abs, the sculpted arms, the way his collar bones stick out just a bit and I want to run my tongue along them.

"That's the thing. I don't think he was," Callan says with a shake of his head. "Nothing serious happened. He came out of the bathroom and stormed out."

"You guys know how he is. He probably had a flashback or something," Lenny adds.

"Flashback? From what?" I ask. My worry is skyrocketing. If he has something going on, then maybe he shouldn't be alone. Especially if he has some form of PTSD. He may really need help.

"It's not our story to tell," Callan answers quickly before anyone else can say anything.

"He's right. Alec will come around eventually. He doesn't have a choice," Maddox says. "He—"

His words are cut off by the loud, old-school phone ring coming from the other room.

"Uh... that's my phone."

I hop off the bed and jog to the other room so I don't miss the call. When I reach it, I wish I hadn't wasted my time. Fuckwad is calling. I thought he'd given up, but I was wrong. I press the fuck you button and go back to the other room where my boys are. My boys? Well, that's new.

As soon as I settle back down between hottie #1 and hottie #2—or should I say 1 and A? Because it's impossible to rank them—it rings again. Once more, he gets the fuck you button. Maddox raises his eyebrows. I shrug in response. When the phone rings a third time, I growl in aggravation, contemplating throwing my phone out the damn window. I'm about to end the call and shut it off when Maddox snatches it from my hand and presses the answer button.

I stare wide-eyed as he brings it to his ear. My body runs cold, worried about what the asshole will say to Maddox.

"Hello? No, she *isn't* available. She's busy. That's none of your goddamn business. Because I said so. Oh, is that so?" A grin slowly forms on his lips, excitement shining in his silver eyes. He turns to me and winks, and my insides swirl with lust. No one has ever done anything like this for me before, and I know that's a stupid thing to be excited about, but having someone stand up for me for once? It's an incredible feeling. "Listen up, shithead, because this is the *one and only* time I'm going to say this. Stop calling Friday's phone, stop texting her, stop doing whatever the fuck it is you're doing and go back to"—he removes the phone from his ear and looks at me, not trying to hide the fact I'm right next to him—"what was her name?"

"Ashley." I say it loud enough so that dickface can hear me. My grin is so big now it hurts.

He puts the phone back to his ear. "That skank Ashley. Trust me, buddy, you don't want to piss me off."

He ends the phone call but doesn't give it back. Instead, he does something I can't see, then I hear the clicking of the camera.

"You're not!" I gasp.

"Oh, I am," he says with a sly grin.

Maddox texts a ridiculously sexy, shirtless selfie to my douchebag ex who is most definitely going to shit himself when he sees who I'm with. Kinda wish I was there to see it.

Chapter Twenty

Lenny

I don't know why we're still moving around if Maddox says Friday is the one. I feel it, and I'm pretty sure Callan feels something. Still, we're packing our things into the Jeep, getting ready to hit the road and move to the next place. When Maddox and I end up alone outside, I decide to ask him. "Why are we moving around if we don't need to? I said I agreed with you. What are we doing?"

"We're not," he says as he tosses our backpacks into the back. "I just don't want to stay in this shithole. Where we go next, it's where we're staying for the rest of the trip."

I wonder why we're still taking this trip at all. Why not just go home?

"Any idea where that will be?"

"Not yet."

"Don't you think you should tell Alec?" He looks at me like I've just asked the single most stupid question possible.

"If you're so worried about it, you do it," he snaps before turning around to go back inside.

Great. He's grumpy today. When I was a kid, I loved watching that Care Bear show. Even then I knew Maddox was the grumpy one, and I was the yellow Funshine one. Although... maybe it's Alec who would have been Grumpy? Not back then, but definitely now. How did I get stuck with two Grumpy Bears?

I finish throwing all the bags I can fit into the Jeep and peek around to make sure Friday isn't nearby. Placing my hand on the inside of the cargo space, I speak a simple incantation to make the space bigger without it appearing larger on the outside of the car. It gives more room to put all our stuff, including Friday's bags. It's convenient, especially when traveling with Callan. He packs enough to stay on the road for six months. Maddox is a close second with all his shit, though no one has the balls to make fun of him.

They are both worried about their appearances too much, but each has a different reason for it. Callan is self-conscious where Maddox is just cocky and *knows* how hot he is. He totally uses it to his advantage, always has. There is a long list of women who would kick him in the balls if given the chance. Some who'd even cut them off and feed them to him. The thought makes me laugh... I can't imagine anyone getting one up on Maddox, but if they all rallied together, they'd get him good.

I've just finished throwing the last of the bags into the cargo space when the guys and Friday file out of the rooms. Closing the door, I hurry to meet Friday. I brush her dark red hair away from her face, and my fingers tingle from the intimate act as I tuck it behind her ear. Her eyes shine in the light, and they look almost cat-like. It's funny how similar they are to Alec's.

She smiles up at me, chewing on her bottom lip.

"Sitting with me?" I ask.

"Of course."

I open the door for her, and she climbs into the middle. I slap her ass playfully as she does, causing her to yelp then giggle. Alec growls before getting in on the other side. I wish he would get over himself already. It would make things so much easier. Though, he's got to give at some point, right? If we keep showing him this is right, maybe he'll cave and give in?

CHAPTER
TWENTY-ONE

FRIDAY

Everyone besides Maddox and I are sleeping. They all went out around the same time, and I find it funny how much they all sleep while in the car. Don't get me wrong, the car soothes me too and I take my fair share of naps, but not as often as them. It's kind of cute.

We've been driving for a while, and I really need to stretch and pee. These car rides are boring as hell, and super uncomfortable. I have no idea why they choose to do this... for fun. Though, it is roomier back here with one less person. It was certainly enough room for six pizza boxes and Lenny and me.

"Tell me about your childhood." Maddox breaks the silence, his voice husky and almost sounding tired. For some reason, he refuses to listen to the radio, which is just ridiculous if you ask me. Who doesn't like music? Especially in the car. I have no idea why he's against it, but I asked him to put it on a little while ago. Lenny shook his head at me while Maddox continued on with his conversation, ignoring me.

"Not much to say really. It was shitty." I look out the window and stare at the trees that pass us. I swear I haven't seen a building in at least two hours.

"Why?" he asks. I glance up to the rearview mirror and see a pair of dark and stormy eyes looking directly at me. There's something in them that I can't describe. My childhood isn't something I like to talk about, but it seems he really wants to know.

I let out a breath before saying, "My mom was, and probably still is, a drug addict. Hardcore. If she isn't dead by now, that is."

"So?"

I grit my teeth, ignoring how rude that was. He is infuriating, though.

"So, she was always high, always fucked up, and always have parties. There were random guys at the house all the time, all hours of the day and night. Every week, I'd wake up to a new guy in her bed and new people passed out on the floor. I'm surprised she kept me alive as a baby, and not getting into her drugs as a toddler was a miracle. Once I was old enough to do things for myself, I did. Mostly because I didn't have a choice. I made meals for myself by five and did my own laundry at seven. Once I got older, her friends started hitting on me and she allowed it. She told me to quit being a prude and learn to live a little. The first time I heard her say that I was only ten. I was thirteen when I got my first job at a local diner, just cleaning up and stuff. I saved every penny minus the bits I took to buy food when there was none in the house because shooting up took priority over feeding your kid. On my sixteenth birthday, I left, knowing there was nothing she could do about it anymore. Though, I don't think she'd have done anything about it at all. The only thing making her want me was whatever money she was getting from the government for me."

"Go on," he urges, though he sounds more interested than concerned. Why the hell does he want to know this so much? Maybe he just wants to get to know me. So, I go on.

"I stayed with this girl from school until I was old enough to get my own apartment. She was a senior who had stayed back and had her own place. I don't think my mother ever looked for me. I stayed in the same town as her so I could continue with school, and she never found me. She was so high all the time, she probably thought she imagined having a kid. After graduation, I moved, finding jobs here and there to keep myself alive. I never had enough money for college or anything like that. My main goal was to survive and stay far away from my mother. I eventually met my ex and well, you know what happened there."

"Right."

He's being weird. This conversation sounded more like an interrogation or a job interview. Not a normal *friendly* conversation, certainly not personal. Though, I've come to expect that from Maddox. It's just who he is. The same way Lenny is the playful one, Callan is the shy one, and Alec is the one who hates me.

Okay, maybe he doesn't hate me, but he definitely doesn't like me. I assumed he'd have come around by now, but nope. He still wants nothing to do with me. You'd think I killed his cat with the way he looks at me. Sure, it's only been a few days, and not everyone is okay having strangers in their space, but he doesn't have to be such an ass about it.

I can't say I regret getting into the car with them, because where else would I be right now? Opening up to Maddox about my childhood felt good. It was also a good reminder of what I'd be walking back into had I chose to go back to my mother instead of these guys. This is a much better option.

But for how long? That's the million-dollar question that I keep ignoring and pushing away.

What is the endgame? When do we part ways? When will they get sick of me mooching off them and tagging along like a desperate little puppy? What do I do when their road trip is done?

I'd thought about this a little before I agreed to come along, and I never got a definitive answer. I have nothing, so I can start from anywhere. Nothing is stopping me from parting ways with them literally anywhere, maybe even where their hometown is. Would that be weird though? I feel like a damn stray dog they picked up on the way, one they'll try to get rid of, but I won't know how to say goodbye because of how well they've taken care of me.

Dammit, that really makes me feel like trash. Fact of the matter is, joining them was my best option at the time. I don't think I'd have done anything differently; I just need to figure out what my next move is before it's too late.

I have a little over two weeks to figure it out. Before their vacation is over, I need a solid plan. That's much better than the short time I had to decide back in Ellbrooke. I think the obvious answer is to start completely new somewhere. The thought of it is exhausting though, I can't imagine actually going through it. But... if it's my only option then I don't have another choice. This could be a good learning opportunity, a chance to get my shit together for once. I've overcome so much in my life so far; I can get past this too. I just need to be smart about it. So far, I think I'm failing at that. I haven't been being smart with these guys, I've been focusing on having fun.

For once in my life, I just want to have fun. I don't want to keep fighting to survive and be happy. Why can't it, just this once, come easily?

My ultimate goal in life is to be everything my mother wasn't. She's the reason I don't want kids, the reason I've never done drugs, and the reason I don't trust anyone completely. If, by chance, I do have kids, I know for sure I'll never do to them what she did to me. I'll do the complete opposite. No fucking way could I ever treat anyone the way she treated me, never mind my own flesh and blood.

Gods, how grateful I am that never happened over the last four years. There were a few scares, but thankfully that's all they were. I can't imagine how much worse things would be right now if that were the case. I'd feel stuck there with him, and I don't think there is anything I hate more than feeling stuck in a situation I can't get out of. I can't ever allow that to happen, which is why I need to gain my independence back and not let it go.

It's okay to have a little fun now, though. As long as I figure out a plan, then I can enjoy the time with the guys. I've already made a few stupid decisions here, but I haven't hurt anyone. I haven't made anything worse. Should I have slept with Lenny? No, probably not, but it's done now. I've always enjoyed sex, so what's wrong with enjoying it now? It was good and I'd definitely do it again. I'm just having a little fun before I have to go back to reality, sort of like my very own vacation.

What happens on the road stays on the road. That totally works, and I'm living by it for the next few weeks. I have nothing to lose. Maybe when this is all said and done, I'll have made a few friends.

I rest my head on Lenny's shoulder and close my eyes. His light snoring lets me know he's still sleeping. He has an airy, nature-like scent that is so refreshing. He smells like mountains and trees, mixed together with sweetness. I breathe him in and open my eyes. I look out the window again, taking in the blue sky. Off in the distance are dark, gray clouds and it looks like we're driving into it. It rains a lot here, and it's then I realize I still don't know where *here* is. I think of asking, but I like the mystery of it. I don't want to know. I'm enjoying just being right now.

An unexpected sadness creeps over me as I watch the cars fly by us on the other side of the highway, and I can't figure out why. Because of life? Of where I am? Being alone? I'm not sure. I can't pinpoint it, but I try not to dwell on it because it isn't important. The car shifts as Maddox veers off the highway onto an exit. He pulls into a gas station, stopping at the pump closest to the door leading to the store.

"Let's go, assholes! Potty break." Maddox slaps Callan on the thigh, the crack booms around the car and I know it hurt. Callan swats at him and growls, then opens the door.

Lenny sucks a deep breath and stretches his arms up, hitting the ceiling. He looks down at me still resting against him and puts his arm around me and hugs me close. His body is warm and firm, and I could really get used to this. Could this be something? I mean, Lenny is definitely silly and fun, but is he trying to have a relationship here? Or is he just messing around? What do I want?

"Aw, you like snuggling?" he asks in this sweet, higher than normal voice. I can't help but laugh. I don't answer because I'm confused by what my answer is. It used to be no. I used to hate cuddling of any kind, but this feels so good.

"As much as I'd like to stay here, I really have to pee," I tell him. "I know I don't have much time before Maddox is yelling at me."

He releases his grip on me. "Maddox can be a real control freak sometimes," he whispers loudly.

"You don't say?" I smirk and wait for him to get out. As he does, Maddox punches him in the shoulder.

"I heard that," he grunts as Alec slides out of the other door. Lenny rubs at the sore spot and just chuckles before offering me his hand and helping me out. I'm sure if Lenny didn't want him to hear it, he wouldn't have.

"It's true and you know it!" Lenny punches him back as Maddox is walking away. He whirls around with a raised brow, challenge in his eye. Lenny runs toward the store before Maddox can get him back. He goes back to pumping the gas and I head into the store myself.

If Maddox and him really went at it, I have a feeling Lenny would be out cold with one punch. Something tells me Maddox would never, not for anything in the world, do that to Lenny though. He may be an asshole, but he's not that much of an asshole.

As we drive deeper into the city, we're met with tall buildings and an obvious city-like atmosphere.

The sun is going down and people are walking around, going in and out of businesses, restaurants, and bars. The sidewalks are lit up with streetlights, music floating through the area from the different establishments. The scent of something sweet, like a bakery, wafts into the car and my mouth starts to water. Lenny said they don't usually stay in places like this because they live in a city, and when they travel, they like to go to the small, lesser-known towns.

My jaw drops when I see the hotel we'll be staying in. Yes, it's an actual hotel this time, and not a dilapidated motel. Surprisingly, it wasn't far from the gas station. I'd never have guessed this beauty was sitting down the hill past the highway.

The outside of the hotel is white and modern, looking brand new. The hotel symbol is printed on the windows in gold—a fancy, scripted S.

Maddox parks along the curb that's allocated for check in, and we get out but leave our bags in the car for now. The doors whoosh open for us as we get closer, and Maddox heads straight to the desk as I stop in the middle of the foyer and look around. The inside is lavish as fuck. The shiny, marble floor has specks of gold and black. There are black statues placed here and there, some have plants around them while others don't. Large gold-framed paintings hang on the walls, mostly abstract. There is even a small set up by the entryway door that has free beverages and snacks. Lenny walks directly to it, and I follow.

Three large glass containers hold water with different fruits floating inside. There are silver trays lined with cookies and muffins. I pluck a sugar cookie off the tray and take a bite—it's not the best cookie I've ever had, but it'll suffice. I take a plastic cup and fill it from the water jug that's flavored with strawberries. Lenny grabs two muffins and a cookie, shoving the entire cookie into his mouth. I glare at him, and he smiles before walking quickly to Maddox and Callan who are still waiting in line to check in. I look around, finding Alec standing outside by himself. My chest squeezes and I take a step toward the door but stop and turn around. He doesn't want anything to do with me, so I just let him be.

By the time I meet the guys, Maddox is taking the key from the tall, skinny blonde behind the counter. She smiles at him with *that look,* and I move closer to Maddox's side, pinning her with a glare. She quickly averts her eyes, bringing her attention to the computer screen. I stand there, not wanting to step away. I know I have no claim over Maddox, but I'll be damned if some girl tries to get her claws into him while I'm here. And when he slides his arm around me, resting his large hand against the bottom of my back, I get dizzy. A wave of warmth rolls through me and I find myself moving even closer to him, sucking in his scent.

"Okay, sir, just sign right here and you're all set." The woman slides the paper toward him, then plucks a pen from the cup and hands it to him with a bright smile. I narrow my eyes at her, but she just keeps staring at him like a desperate wench.

Maddox removes his arm from around me to sign the paper, and without a word to her, he turns and faces Lenny.

"Go get Alec. We'll meet you upstairs."

Lenny nods and winks as he moves by me. I watch as he goes out the door to get Alec until someone is gripping my hand and pulling me toward the elevator. I glance at that tattooed hand, follow it up the thick forearm all the way to Maddox's smirking face. I glance over my shoulder at the woman behind the desk who's watching me, green with envy. I smile at her, then turn to face forward again.

We reach the top floor and step off the elevator. The sign on the wall in front of us lists only two rooms on this floor, one to the right and one to the left. We go right, toward the Luxury Suite. I raise a brow.

"We're staying in a suite?" I question as we reach the door. Maddox swipes the card and glances at me, he doesn't answer. He pushes the door open, standing aside to let me in. My eyes roam over every inch of the place as I make my way inside, unable to believe *this* is where we are staying. "What do you do to be able to afford a place like this?" I ask in awe.

"Wouldn't you like to know?" He's being cocky, repeating the first words I ever spoke to him. He's teasing me and I know I won't get an answer from him now, so I may as well just ignore him. I'll ask Lenny later.

The first room we walk into is the kitchen. It's a full kitchen with normal sized, stainless-steel appliances. The floor is white tile with black grout that matches the backsplash behind the countertops that are gray and white marble. The cabinetry is all white and solid wood. There's a round glass table off to the side with four chairs around it. Further ahead is a living room with a large TV and two couches facing each other. A long line of drapes off to the right of the room has me thinking there's a balcony there, or at least floor to ceiling windows.

Between the kitchen and living room is the entry to the hallway, which is to the right, and then the bathroom door to the left. The bathroom is your standard hotel bathroom. Everything is white, even the shower curtain to the large bath and shower combo. The mirror is large and spotless, and there is so much counter space in here.

I move down the hallway and find three bedrooms, each with only one bed. Since there are five of us, someone will be sharing a room. Unless both of the couches are pull-outs, which I doubt. Maybe one of them will be? Though, someone could just sleep on the couch as is.

The faint beeping of the door being unlocked pulls me back down the hallway, and I find Lenny and Alec walking in with a trolley piled high with our belongings. I still have no idea how Lenny manages to fit all of that stuff in the trunk. He must be really good at Tetris. He starts to unload the bags, leaving them between the kitchen and living room before placing the trolley outside the door.

"Sleeping arrangements? There're only three beds." I look between everyone as I reach the pile of bags. We're all glancing over everything, and I wonder who is going to dig in first.

"Actually, there are five. Both sofas have a pull-out," Maddox says, flashing me a grin. "But if you want to share a bed with me, I won't say no."

I scoff and flip him off. "You wish."

Alec shakes his head before digging through the bags and pulling out a black duffle and a backpack. He walks down the hall and goes into the only room on the right, closing the door harshly behind him.

"Looks like he found his room," I say, planting my hands on my hips. "I'll sleep on the couch."

"Hogwash!" Lenny shouts, and we all turn to stare at him with confusion. "What? It's a good word." He throws his hands up, like we are the weird ones here. Who says that anymore? All I can do is laugh because how do you answer that?

"Callan and Lenny will sleep on the sofas. You have a room." There he goes again, bossing everyone around. And there I go… soaking my panties.

"But this is *your* vacation," I argue. "I should—" Maddox holds up his hand to silence me, and dammit, why do I snap my mouth shut? I narrow my eyes at him, and neither of us says another word.

"Please, allow me to assist with your bags, my lovely lady," Lenny drawls, pulling my attention from Maddox's gray eyes. Lenny snatches up my bags, and as I watch him move down the hall, I realize I don't think I'd ever get sick of having him around. He's thoughtful, helpful, sweet, funny, and good in bed. Isn't that like, the ultimate list for a boyfriend?

"Lenny, quit the shit," Maddox calls after him.

"Maddox, quit being jealous!" he responds.

He stops in front of the two rooms, the doors only a few feet apart. When I reach his side, he asks, "Which one do you want?" I take a peek into each room again. They're both set up pretty much the same way, the biggest difference are the colors. One is decorated in shades of blue while the other is shades of red, but also kind of pink.

"This one!" I say excitedly.

"I was hoping you'd say that." He grins.
Payback in small amounts.

CHAPTER TWENTY-TWO

FRIDAY

It's close to nine when Maddox tells me we're going out. He assures me bars around here don't close until at least two, even on a Sunday. *He* decided we were going to have a night out tonight. After coming into my room and very sarcastically thanking me for the room I left him with, he announced we were going out and to dress up nicely. He also let me know I could unpack because we will be staying here for more than a few days. I asked him why, since I know the point in their trip is traveling around and the only answer I got was some kind of mumble about it being cheaper or something.

Whatever. It doesn't matter to me. I'm just happy they're still letting me tag along.

Dumping everything in my bags onto the floor, I start digging through. I go through and start sorting things while also looking for something to wear. I toss shirts to the right, pants to the left, underwear in front of me, and everything else behind me. I come across a few dresses that I place right on my side, and once I have a good pile, I lay them out on the bed and decide on a tight, black dress with a square neckline that makes my hips look amazing. I saw an iron in the closet, thankfully, because all of these clothes are wrinkled to hell.

I don't have many shoes with me, and only two pairs that would match the dress. I decide on the heels I swore I would never wear again, because they match the best. I should have burned them. Maybe I still will. They're exceptionally comfortable when used appropriately, but they aren't meant to walk miles in.

Before getting dressed, I shower and spend a half-hour in the bathroom fixing my hair and doing my make-up. I don't usually spend this much time on that kind of stuff, but something about going out with these guys tonight makes me want to look good... *really good*, and for a couple of reasons.

One: intimidation. If we are going out to a club, there will be girls everywhere. Even though these guys aren't *technically* mine, it's still hands-off... from the other girls, of course, not me. The better I can look, the more likely they won't try anything with me around.

Two: attention. Maybe Alec and Callan won't acknowledge how I look, but Lenny and Maddox will. Maddox won't come out and say anything, but he has this look in his eye that he gives me when he likes what he sees. I know he wants me, probably not as badly as I want him, but it's still there. I like that feeling, like knowing I'm being lusted after. After being cheated on, the attention feels good. I am only human, after all, and I never said

I was perfect. With any luck, Lenny won't keep his hands to himself.

Three: confidence. When you feel that you look good, you're in a better mood. I want to have a good night tonight. I want to have fun. Who knows when I will ever have something like this again? A night out with a bunch of hot guys? With friends? I don't want anything to ruin it, and the more comfortable I am in how I look, the better the night will go.

After my hair and make-up are done, I saunter toward my bedroom wearing nothing but a towel. Maddox, Lenny, and Callan are all in the living room. I don't spare them a glance as I pass by, but I feel all three of them staring at me. And damn, does it feel good.

When I reach my room, I pat myself on the back for a job well done. Get them interested now, so they'll be anticipating my being dressed up.

Closing the door behind me, I drop the towel and slip into my little black dress. No bra, no panties. You can't wear those things with a dress like this, and if the guys notice it? Bonus points.

"Hurry up, or we will leave without you," Maddox threatens from the other side of the door.

Liars. They would do no such thing.

Would they? I should hurry up just in case they do.

Not wanting to carry a purse, I pull my ID out of my wallet and grab a couple of twenties. I throw my purse into the closet and shut the doors, then I leave my phone on the bedside table since I really don't need it for anything. I take one more look in the mirror, fluffing my hair and giving my boobs a lift before slipping on my shoes and heading down the hall.

The three of them are waiting in the living room when I get there, standing in a half-circle, sharing small talk. Fuck me, they all look good enough to eat.

I stop at the end of the hallway and just take them in. Maddox has on light jeans that hug his thick thighs all too well, even showing off his impressive bulge that I stare at for way too long. The navy button up fits him just as well, looking as if it may tear if he moves too quickly. The sleeves are rolled up, and I know he did that on purpose. His face is freshly shaven, his hair perfectly styled neat and short.

Lenny has on dark khaki chinos with a white button-up shirt. His sleeves are also rolled up. If I don't start drooling in a second, I'll be surprised. His hair is pulled back in the purposely messy sort of way he gets perfect every time. I've never seen a bit of hair on his face, and that's no different now.

Callan is dressed in navy blue pants, a white button-up, and a maroon vest. If his sleeves were rolled up, I'm sure I'd lose it. Something about that nerdy, well-dressed look really gets me going. His hair is perfectly styled in a short pompadour. His face is covered in a light stubble that I would love to feel between my thighs.

I realize I've been staring for way too long, and I can't believe no one has called me out on it. I shake myself out of it and move forward, holding out my ID.

"Can someone hold this for me?" I look between the three of them, and no one answers me.

"Well?"

"You look fucking hot," Lenny says, his bright blue eyes looking me up and down.

Well, I guess that's why they didn't call me out on staring at them. They were doing the same damn thing to me. My cheeks flush and I tuck some hair behind my ear.

"Thanks, Lenny. So do you." I wink at him and smile. He bites his lip in return, letting out a grunt. If there was any question about how tonight was going to go, they have all been answered with the looks I'm getting from them. Actually, I'm pretty sure they all have boners.

One point for Friday. Nah, make it ten. Ten *each.*

I turn my attention to Maddox, who has the equivalent of resting bitch face for men etched on his beautiful face. I wait on bated breath, hoping he's going to give me a compliment. Something as simple as saying I look pretty. He doesn't though, and instead of upsetting me, it only makes me want to push him more until he does.

"Put your money away. Give me your ID." Maddox snatches the ID from me and puts it into his wallet that he pulls from his back pocket.

"Just take the money for my drinks." I shove it at him, and he lets out a low laugh, one that holds more than an ounce of condescension and has me feeling a little self-conscious.

"Friday, put your money away." He speaks the words slowly, but less cocky and a little more genuine. Is that him trying to be nice?

I let out a huff, and go back to my room to put the money away. When I walk back out, Maddox is banging on Alec's door.

"Let's go, asshole. We're leaving!" he shouts.

Wow, I didn't think he would be coming with us. Actually, even with Maddox banging on the door I don't think Alec will open it. I mean, why would he come with us? He seems like he wants nothing to do with anyone. I've quickly learned I'm not the only one he ignores. He doesn't seem to talk to anyone.

A moment later the door opens, and I'm proven wrong. Alec walks out, looking sexy as fuck. Damn... why does he have to hate me? He gives me a quick look, his eyes widening a fraction before he turns his gaze away and moves down the hall. He's in dark jeans, that make his ass look so good, and a maroon button up. Maddox moves after him, and I follow them both.

Alec is the first one out the room door, and the rest of us follow behind. As we walk, Maddox places his hand on my lower back again, causing a shiver to run through me. Even as it dissipates, my skin tingles where his hand lingers, hot and gentle. The light is on as we reach the elevator, and it reaches our floor a moment later. No one says anything as we make our way down, and it's only when we're just about at the exit doors that someone says something.

"Are we getting a taxi?" Callan asks, slipping his hands into his pockets.

"No, we aren't going far." Maddox leads the way, still guiding me along with him. We turn right and move down the sidewalk, moving through people as we go. Lenny moves to my left side and takes my hand, interlocking our fingers. His sweetness warms my heart, bringing a smile to my face. For a split second, I wonder what people think as they see me walking like this with two guys, both with their hands on me in some sort of way. I'm not worried about being judged, in fact, it makes me feel good. I feel powerful.

The town really comes alive at night. The sidewalks are filled with people the further away from the hotel we walk. Everyone is dressed nicely, looking like they're enjoying a night out. The streets are lit brightly by the tall streetlights, and signs glow brightly above the businesses, indicating what can be found inside. The energy is lively, and I love it.

We walk three blocks before stopping at a building settled between two larger ones. The top two floors are lined with glass windows. Inside, people are dancing and drinking. Bright flashing lights illuminate the area around us in different colors. The heavy bass of the music booms all the way out here, and I can't wait to be inside and feel it vibrate through my body.

We get in line and wait only a moment before it starts to move. When we reach the end, the bouncer, a tall dark-skinned man dressed in all black and sunglasses—even though it's night-time—asks us for our ID's. Maddox shows him mine and his, then the other guys give him theirs. Once he checks them all, he removes the red rope, allowing us to pass by. We walk through one door and are stopped once again. This time, it's a girl about my age, dressed in nothing but a bright red, sparkly bra and matching panties. Her bleach-blonde hair is up in a messy bun, with a few short curls falling down beside her face. She tells us there's a cover charge, and Maddox hands over his credit card to pay for everyone.

I haven't seen anyone other than him pay for a damn thing. Now I really want to know what he does for work... what if he's a hitman or some kind of mob boss? God, that would be just my luck to get involved with someone like that.

We follow Maddox's lead as he heads up the stairs. I'm directly behind him, with Lenny behind me. This first floor seems like more of a leisurely hangout; it's dark and there's a few TV's hanging on the walls. There are tables throughout, not enough room to dance anywhere. Once we get to the second landing, I know instantly this is where the club is at. The bright colored strobe lights cause everyone in front of me to look like nothing more than dark silhouettes. The energy alone makes me want to dance, but I decide to wait.

We head to the bar and Maddox orders us all drinks. I can't hear what he says to the bartender because the music is too loud, but I'll drink anything at this point. The bartender slides five shot glasses in front of Maddox, and fills them with whisky... so, this is how the night is going? Guess there's no point in wasting time, may as well get drunk right away. Maddox passes us each a glass and holds it up, we clink them together, Lenny and I giving a little whoop, and then we take them. The bartender clears the counter of the empty glasses with one hand, while pouring alcohol into a cup with the other. A moment later, we all have a drink in our hands, and I'm pleased when I taste vodka and soda. It's what I was drinking the other night, and I like knowing he was paying attention. Everyone seems to have a different drink in their hands. Maddox and Alec both have some dark liquid with no ice, while Callan's is clear with no ice, and Lenny's is some kind of mixed drink like mine, only it's garnished with a cherry and mine wasn't.

We find an empty table in one of the back corners and sit. It's too loud to share conversation, so we just sip our drinks and listen to the music. I drink mine quickly and hold the empty cup out to Maddox. He waves his hand at a passing waitress who's wearing fishnets, a black thong and black corset. Her dark hair is pulled back in a sleek and shiny ponytail. Honestly, she's hot as hell. She comes over to the table, and Maddox orders me another drink. She barely pays him any attention, just jots the drink onto her notepad then moves to the next table. She returns a few minutes later with my drink, sliding it over to me and smiles.

I'm on my third drink when I can't sit still anymore. The alcohol is making its way through my body, and it feels so damn good.

The loud, pounding of the bass vibrates through my body and I have the sudden urge to dance. I finish my drink and make eye contact with Maddox as I get up from the table. He holds my gaze, his eyes dark as I saunter toward the dance floor. I keep eye contact for as long as I can, but even after I break it, I still feel his eyes on me.

I move into the crowd, merging in with the other drunk people and start to move my body along to the fast beat. I've never been shy or embarrassed about dancing. I'm not great at it, but I love it anyway. Besides, it doesn't matter how good I am at it because I'm drunk, and I bet everyone around me is too.

Bodies are pressed all around me as I sway to the music. My eyes fall shut as I feel the music, letting the rhythm guide my movements. For the first time in a long time, I feel so damn good. I'm happy, without a care in the world.

I don't know how long I'm out here for before there's a warm, hard body stepping behind me. I look down as an arm hooks around my waist, and the tattoos give away who it is immediately. He presses his front to my back, his hand sliding down to my hip, and then back over my stomach that twists under the gentle brush of his fingers. I push my ass into him, certain I feel his dick harden. With the alcohol in my system, my need to make Maddox beg for me is out the window.

I lift my arm and wrap it around the back of his neck as we rock side to side to an EDM remix of a song I can't recall the name of. His mouth finds my throat, but he doesn't kiss me. He drags his lips up the length of my neck, his hot breath causing goosebumps. Maddox's hand tightens around me, and he groans in my ear. My stomach flips at the husky sound. I spin in his arms, bringing mine back up and around his neck, before lifting up on my toes and kissing him. I pull my lips away but drag my tongue along his bottom one before nipping at it when he does nothing in response. I sink my teeth in harder and finally earn a growl, which has him pressing forward and owning my mouth. His soft, velvety tongue slides across mine slowly, but with firm strokes.

I'm lost in him. The feel of his body, his mouth, his scent. It's just him.

My hands find his face and I grip him tightly as I push for more, grinding against him and sucking on his tongue.

His lips go to my neck, I move my head to the side allowing him more access. He licks, sucks, and bites my neck, all the while we still dance to the music, moving our bodies in sync. With his arms around me, I feel protected. I feel safe and cherished. I feel wanted. Even if he doesn't use his words, I feel his need for me, especially now, with his hands moving lower and lower to grasp my ass. I start to let go of the control I've been holding on to and allow him to take over completely. The song ends and another starts. Then another and another, and still we're going at each other like young lovers who just can't get enough. We're both hot and sweaty, and it only makes the situation sexier.

Someone comes up behind me, and I don't have to look to know who it is. Somehow, I just know. *I feel him.* Lenny brings a drink to my mouth, and I find the straw with my lips as Maddox lessens his kisses to my throat, and instead moves them along my shoulder. I suck down half the vodka and soda before releasing the straw, and Lenny pulls it away. I spin to face him, not hesitating to find his lips. Unlike Maddox, he doesn't tease me, doesn't hesitate.

His tongue immediately goes into my mouth, the sharp taste of whiskey on his breath. It tastes delicious; he tastes delicious. God, everything about this night is perfect. Lenny's hands are in my hair, while Maddox's are still wrapped firmly around my waist, and it seems he has no intention of letting go. Somehow, the three of us manage to move together in the most amazing way, like we've been doing this for years.

It seems like hours pass as we dance together, and I go back and forth between making out with them. My pussy is aching and dripping wet at the thought of this continuing back in the hotel room. There isn't a single part of me that cares what anyone is thinking. These guys make me feel amazing, they make me feel real, like I'm worth something. It's an unfamiliar feeling, new and strange. It's also addicting, so damn addicting, and I can't get enough. Which is why I'm going to keep this going as long as I can.

I slide my hand behind my back and reach for Maddox's cock, giving it a firm squeeze. He releases a breathy moan in my ear, and I smile against Lenny's lips.

Maddox slides his fingers up the outside of my thigh, hooking his fingers into the hem of my dress when he reaches it. He slides his fingers forward over my thigh, so damn close to where I want him to touch me. He drags his finger back and forth as I run my hand along his erection.

"Let's get another shot," Maddox whispers in my ear.

I don't need one, but I want one. Also, we should probably take a break from each other before I try getting him to fuck me right here in the middle of the dance floor. I nod and he steps away, which gives me room to step back from Lenny. I smile up at him as I take his hand and pull him after Maddox who is waving Callan and Alec over to the bar.

After another round of shots and another drink, I make my way back to the dance floor. My body is buzzing, warm, and feeling so damn good. Lenny finds me right away and starts to dance with me again. I look around through foggy vision and can't find Maddox anywhere, but I do spot Callan walking over with a drink in each hand. I don't know what comes over me, but as I reach for the drink he's offering me, I lean in and crash my lips to his.

I can't help myself.

I'm drunk.

I'm horny.

Callan is hot as fuck.

He freezes, his whole body going stiff. My tongue traces the seam of his lips, but he pulls away, the other drink in his hand crashing to the floor and splashing everyone's feet with the cool liquid. No one but me and Lenny seem to notice, and when I look back up, I find Callan rushing toward the exit and disappearing down the stairs.

CHAPTER TWENTY-THREE

FRIDAY

Okay, so maybe I fucked up, but is it really that serious? Does he not know how to have a little bit of fun? It was just a kiss. I mean, strangers do more! I haven't been around long, but it's been long enough. I didn't go anywhere near his dick, and if he didn't want to kiss me, he could have just stopped it and told me no. He didn't have to run away like that. Which is why, and I thank the alcohol, I chase after him. Clearly about to make things worse. I hand my drink to Lenny, who stands there shell shocked as I go after Callan. Moving as fast as I can in these stupid heels, I spot him as he's pushing through the door to outside. Much to my amazement, I catch up to him not far from the front door.

"What is your problem? Do you have a girlfriend or something?" I demand as I reach his side and grab onto his arm. Thankfully, I don't have to fight with him to stop and he just does. My chest is tight, and my head is swimming from all the alcohol.

"No, Friday. That's not it," he says, his tone impatient. He shoves his hands into his pockets and stares at me with this look that I can't figure out.

"Then what? What is wrong with me? I don't get it." Tears sting at my eyes, and I have no idea why. What the hell is wrong with me?

"There is nothing wrong with you," he assures me.

"Then what?" I wipe a tear away, pissed that this is happening. The night was going too well, I should have known it wouldn't stay that way. "I know you barely know me, but I'm just trying to have fun, I'm just—"

"I'm a virgin, okay?" The words come out harsh, tinged with embarrassment. He shakes his head and then starts walking again. It takes me too long to realize what just came out of his mouth, and he's already halfway down the block.

"But you said…" I mumble the words to myself, staring at the ground as I'm filled with confusion. I turn back to him, and then hurry after him again. How is he a virgin? It doesn't make sense "You said!" I call after him, and he stops abruptly causing me to bump into him.

"I lied," he says sharply. "Okay? I don't like putting my business out there. And you're right. I know you're just trying to have fun, and I probably should lighten up a little, but this whole thing is out of my comfort zone. These vacations are normally just guys and—"

"Well, I'm so sorry to have ruined your vacation!" I shout in his face, and then I'm the one who stomps off. Why? Because

I'm drunk and being irrational. I have no right to be upset with him, I know that, but I can't help it.

My heels clack on the cement and I swear I'm burning them to a crisp the second I can because they're bad luck. They have to be! The night was going so well... I wrap my arms around myself as I keep walking, remembering the club was a straight walk from the hotel, so if I just keep going this way, I should get back there...

"Hey," Lenny's smooth voice sounds in my ear as he puts his arm around my shoulder. "Come on, let's go back to the hotel." His body keeps me warm as the chilly air breezes against my skin, and I'm so grateful for him right now. But the more we walk, the more guilty I feel over ruining the night. What the hell is wrong with me? Why did I have to do that? Callan did nothing to make me think he wanted me to kiss him, so why the hell did I do it? If the tables were turned, I'd be just as pissed as he was. My god, I am so stupid.

When we get to the hotel, Lenny takes my hand and pulls me to a bench just inside the foyer. He places his hands on my upper arms, rubbing up and down. "You okay?" he asks.

I nod. "Yeah, just... I don't know." I shrug, not sure how I'm feeling other than confused, a little angry with myself, and a whole lot of numb. Lenny pulls me into a hug, wrapping his arms around me and holding me tight. Being here, like this, it feels so good. The more it happens, the more I don't want it to end, yet I know it will. That only makes my mood worse.

When we get back to the room, Callan is lying on one of the couches with his arm draped over his face. I want to apologize but figure now isn't the time. I assume Maddox and Alec are in their rooms because I don't see them anywhere. Lenny walks me to my room and when he doesn't step inside, I grab his hand and pull.

I realize just how messed up I am when I'm leaning up to kiss him. After all that happened, and I'm still acting this way? Why? Am I truly this messed up as a person? Or maybe I'm just so numb and need to feel something... but why?

Lenny's hands go to my ass, and he squeezes, pulling me close to him as he kisses me back. I moan into his mouth and slide my hands down his chest to grip his shirt before I grasp at the buttons and start to undo them. He spins us around and pushes me against the wall as his hands move up my sides. My fingers fumble with the buttons of his shirt but I finally get them all undone. He's wearing a white undershirt beneath, and I slide my hands under it and up his abs. His body is so warm, so smooth and god, I am aching so badly.

I grab his wrist and bring it between my legs, not wanting to wait anymore. He tugs my dress up and then slides his fingers over my pussy, groaning when he feels how wet I am. He starts to circle my clit, and my head falls against the wall with a thud. He boxes me in with his hand against the wall as the other strokes my clit. I spread my legs wider, rocking my hips against his hand.

"Fuck, you're so sexy," he breathes out.

I open my eyes and meet his, bright and heated. I lick my lips and my eyes fall shut again as the pleasure builds. I'm so close, right there, about to come when he stops and steps back.

Lenny's knee goes between my legs to spread them wider. One hand still gripping my ass while the other builds up an orgasm I really need right now. His mouth moves to my neck, sucking and licking my sensitive flesh. Right when I am at the point of no return, he stops and backs up.

"Fuck, don't stop," I groan. "Why are you stopping?" I'm about ready to beg him to keep going, to please make me come. I don't want him to stop.

The response I get is a smirk. God, the anger that rushes through me is so uncalled for, but dammit, I just want to come already! It's been hours of build up between him and Maddox, I just need this.

Lenny takes his button up off, dropping it to the floor before tugging the other over his head and tossing it away too. He takes a few more steps back, and I'm not letting him get away with this so easily. Only when I step forward, I notice Maddox standing in the doorway. I narrow my eyes at Lenny, whose smirk turns into a grin, but instead of chasing him, I spin and lunge toward Maddox. I throw my arms around his neck and bring my lips to his.

The two of them are so different. Maddox is harsh and rough, while Lenny is teasing and playful.

I run my hands along his shoulder before sliding down his arms, feeling the curve of muscles beneath my palms. I'd anticipated having to work harder for this, but when Maddox lifts me up and walks us toward the bed, I'm so relieved. God, yes, please! Please let this be it.

Maddox lays me onto the bed, his body hovering over mine. He pulls back, and when he steps away, I groan loudly. My chest is heaving for breath, my pussy literally aching with the need to come.

Lenny is down to his briefs, and Maddox is well on his way. The sight of them has me momentarily distracted and I find myself wanting to watch them do whatever it is they plan to do. Lenny gives Maddox a look I can't figure out, but I quickly forget about it when Lenny is moving toward me. Maddox steps in front of him though, blocking his path. He grips him by the back of the neck and pulls him into a kiss that has my entire body alight with fire. Their kiss is slow but rough, Maddox holding Lenny still with a hand on his throat, clearly taking the lead. Lenny's fingers dig into Maddox's arms, and he groans under his breath, moving closer and kissing him harder.

Maddox's free hand finds Lenny's dick, and he squeezes causing Lenny to buck his hips and groan. He slips his hand inside the material and pushes it down while circling Lenny's dick, stroking him slowly. The muscles in Lenny's legs twitch as he gives into the pleasure, and I find myself wanting to join them so fucking badly, but I can't seem to move. I'm stunned, frozen in place, as I watch them share something so intimate... intimate, yet I know they're doing it on purpose. Clearly they're trying to kill me.

When Maddox starts to jerk Lenny off at a much quicker pace, I'm pulled out of whatever shock I'm in, get up from the bed and drop to my knees between them. I hook my fingers into the waistband of Maddox's briefs and tug them down. His dick is so hard and dripping at the tip. I grasp him by the base and swirl my tongue around the tip, licking up his flavor. He groans this deep, rumbling sound that has me sucking harder and taking him deeper into my throat. I'm suddenly more focused on wanting him to come than myself.

Maddox is thick, but I take as much of him as I can. The deeper he goes, the sexier the sounds he makes. He pulses and throbs, growing impossibly harder as his hips start to move, thrusting into my mouth.

A hand on my back has me opening my eyes and glancing up, only to find Maddox looking down at me, face twisted into pleasure. His hand comes down to rest on the back of my head as he slowly pushes forward. He hits the back of my throat and pauses for a few seconds before pulling out. He does this over and over, moving so slowly but seemingly enjoying every bit. I've never enjoyed sucking someone's dick as much as I'm enjoying this right now. Everything about the way he's acting shows me how much he enjoys it and that has me feeling something I can't put into words.

Lenny pushes my dress up around my waist before running his hands over the curve of my ass. His fingers are at my pussy again, dragging his fingers along my soaked slit and I moan around Maddox's dick, which he seems to enjoy if the shiver I feel from him is any indication.

Lenny circles my clit, and my moans grow louder and closer together. Maddox takes complete control now, placing both hands on my face as he fucks me. He's careful but rough at the same time, taking what he needs but not wanting to hurt me.

Pleasure swirls in my belly as Lenny gives all his attention to my clit, stroking me in the best possible way. I try pulling Maddox's dick out of my mouth, wanting to tell them I'm going to come, but he doesn't allow it. He grunts out a sound of disapproval before fucking me faster. My breathing grows erratic as I fight for air around his dick, my fingers digging into his thighs. The orgasm takes me over and I cry out a choked sound, my body shaking with wave after wave of mind-shattering bliss.

Before I know what's happening, Maddox is pulling out of me and I'm being flipped over onto my back, the carpet soft beneath me.

Lenny is on his knees beside me, and I reach for him, wanting more, but it's Maddox who ends up between my legs. "You've been waiting for this," Maddox says as he strokes himself a few times, using his other hand to spread my legs wide open and look down at me.

I moan out a yes, not caring that I'm once again not making him work for a damn thing. I just want him inside of me.

My response must please him, because he lines himself up and slides in. A low groan leaves him, his eyes falling shut. I lift my hips, hoping he'll push in even deeper, and when he does, my body shivers in delight. Maddox starts to fuck me in long, rough strokes, his hips slamming against me as he goes as deep as he can each and every time. He holds onto my hips, keeping me in place and I grip onto his arms, needing something to hold. Lenny watches us the entire time, stroking himself as he watches Maddox fuck me.

Another orgasm hits me out of nowhere, and I'm blinded with bright spots behind my eyes, my body tensing, pussy clenching around Maddox.

"Fucking Christ..." Maddox starts to fuck me harder, my orgasm seeming to never end.

"You coming?" Lenny asks breathlessly, and I know he isn't asking me.

Maddox grunts out a yes right before his fingers are bruising my skin, holding me to him as he releases inside me. I feel every pulse, every throb of his thick cock, and as if that isn't hot enough, Lenny groans next, releasing on my stomach as he strokes himself.

Fuck hell if this isn't the best night of my life.

CHAPTER TWENTY-FOUR

CALLAN

Why did I have to be so senseless? I had my opportunity, and I ruined it. Not the opportunity to lose my virginity, I don't care about that. There is a reason I haven't had sex yet. It's not because I didn't have the chance—I've had many. I'm the only one who has taken this mate thing so seriously throughout the years, and that's why I've chosen not to give that part of me to anyone else. The other guys, though? Sure, they take it seriously now, but they didn't when we were younger. They weren't thinking about our future and the woman we would be with. They didn't think about her feelings. They let their hormones get in the way and couldn't care less about what our future mate would think. I did—I always did, and I still do. Especially now. Looking at Friday, being around her...

I'm glad I waited because it was for *her*.

I ruined my chance of crossing the boundaries I've built over the years. My "comfort hump," as I call it. We all have a comfort zone, anxieties, worries, and things of the like. The comfort hump is the invisible line between anxiety and comfort. For me, taking the leap over that line is easier when I'm forced into things unexpectedly, like I was earlier at the club. There was no time to think, no time to worry because what I was anxious about was already happening. I should have gone with it, kept it going, kissed her back. Gods, I should have kissed her back.

The lack of experience I have with women has always been a touchy subject for me. I'm not big on social situations, and when people find that out about me, it only makes them talk more. I usually want them to talk less. Friday opened up the perfect window for me to jump through, and she opened it so quickly. I regret what I did. I shouldn't have acted the way I did, not only in the club, but afterwards too.

She followed me, clearly feeling apologetic. I shouldn't have raised my voice at her, but I was just so uncomfortable in my own skin at that point. It was a reaction to how I was feeling, and not her. So, in turn, I upset her, which I hate.

It could be me in the room with her right now. Either with the other guys... or alone. I could have had her in the club had I gone along with it. I wanted to, so badly. I was watching her the entire time she was dancing with Lenny and Maddox, wishing it were me she was rubbing her ass against, or me she was tasting. But those two lucky, outspoken jerks get all the fun. It's so damn easy for them. They're both so charming and pleasant. Sometimes it sucks to be me. Sometimes I wish I could be more like them, but there's like an invisible wall that goes up anytime speaking is involved. It's a miracle I've made it as a teacher this long.

The sounds coming from her room only make me feel worse. I want to get up and go in there. I want to join in, to make her mine as much as she is theirs, but I can't do it. They would let me; I know they would. But the thought of it... it's too much.

One day, I'll have to suck it up. But one day will be the right day. It'll happen when it's supposed to happen. That's what I tell myself, so I don't feel like a complete failure.

I try to envision what's going on in that room... my imagination is running wild with the possibilities. The thought of going in there, or her putting her soft lips on mine has me hard and aching. Gods, I haven't wanted to get off this badly in years.

I unbutton my pants and slip my hand inside, running my fingertips along my length. I swallow hard as the slightest pressure from my hand has me pulsing with need. It sends sharp pleasure up through my stomach and I wrap my hand around myself and squeeze.

Moans and grunts come from Friday's room, and I picture her moaning for me. I imagine it's her hand stroking me right now, my hips naturally moving with the rhythm of my hand. What are the guys doing to her? Are they doing anything together? Would they do that? Would she be okay with that?

I rub myself harder and faster, my hips grinding into my hand, only stopping when the orgasm hits. I squeeze my cock, feeling it pulse in my fist as my cum fills the inside of my briefs. I release a deep, breathy moan, immediately hoping it wasn't too loud. I cannot get caught doing this.

Who am I kidding? They're too occupied to worry about me.

I look down at my pants and find the evidence has soaked through my pants, and there is now a wet spot. I lay my head back and stare at the ceiling as I try to catch my breath. When

the sounds in the other room grow silent, I know it's time to get
up and shower before someone finds me like this.

CHAPTER
TWENTY-FIVE

MADDOX

The sun is barely peeking through the blinds when Lenny sneaks into my room. He climbs into my bed, and I hit him with my pillow and yell at him to get out. I'm exhausted today, probably because I haven't been sleeping well. I go through stages of it, and always figured it was a vampire thing.

"Maddox, it's Monday morning. Get up." He taps my bare shoulder. "We gotta do this before Friday wakes up."

It takes me a minute to realize what he's talking about.

"It's not even your turn, Lenny. Go away," I mumble into the pillow, swatting blindly at him.

"Do you really trust Alec with this right now?"

"Go wake up Callan."

"Just get up and let's get this over with," he grunts.

Lenny does this every week for me, it's one of the reasons our bond is so strong. Of course, it's easier with him because we live so close. It's not worth my time to drive to the others just to feed.

I am a vampire, and I have urges and needs. The best way to keep me sharp is with weekly feedings. Not all vampires need that to sustain themselves, it's different for everyone. Some need more and some need less. Over the years, I've found this is what works for me, and collectively, we've come up with a set of rules because I wasn't so in control of my blood lust.

One of the first rules is that the guys swap out whenever they can. Lenny gets a break when the others are around because this takes a toll on him week after week, especially when his mood isn't great—which happens sometimes. Most of the time Lenny is happy-go-lucky, but he goes through these phases when he's the complete opposite.

"No, get out and let me sleep," I groan, knowing it isn't fair for him to be the only one who does this for me. He says he doesn't care, and maybe he doesn't, but I do.

"Whatever then, be a grumpy bitch." The bed dips as he climbs off, and then he's out of my room and I fall right back to sleep.

"Hey, Maddox?" Callan whispers, waking me up. It feels like it's been mere minutes since Lenny left.

"What do you want, Callan?" I mumble into the pillow, too tired to move.

"Uh, can we talk?"

I groan at the question.

"Does it have to be right now? Kinda sleeping here."

"I suppose not." The soft click of the door tells me he leaves and I once again drift back to sleep.

A soft knocking on my door wakes me up this time, once again after what feels like mere minutes.

"Is this a fucking joke?" I growl into the pillow. "I'm trying to sleep!"

"Well, you don't have to be such a dick about it! I was just bringing you food." Friday actually sounds upset at that, though the emotion is hidden under the sass.

Shit.

I force myself out of bed and to the door, but when I open it, there is no one there. I step into the hallway, not caring I'm buck ass naked. The scent of dough fills the air and I realize how hungry I am. What time is it? When I reach the kitchen, I find her standing in front of the stove, moving something around with a spatula. Callan and Lenny are at the table, both with plates piled high with pancakes.

"Gods, Maddox, could you put some pants on?" Callan's cheeks turn red, and he dips his head to stare at his food.

"Come on, Callan, you know you like looking at my cock." I grin.

"You wish," he mumbles.

I turn toward Friday, taking a few steps closer to her, but also keeping my distance. I'd prefer to stay away from fire when my dick is out in the open.

"Where's my food, beautiful?"

"I gave them to Lenny and Callan, the guys who weren't rude."

"Oh, chill out. You can't expect a guy to be nice when he's woken up. Are you making more?"

"Only if you ask nicely," she sing-songs.

Lenny snickers from the table. I flip my middle finger at him, not bothering to turn around.

I watch her with narrowed eyes, taking in the curve of her ass and the swell of her tits, remembering how god damn beautiful she looked beneath me last night.

"Please?" I grunt. Fuck, that was not easy. She turns to stare at me, hand on her hip and the other one holding the spatula. She purses her lips, and I know immediately my "nice" wasn't nice enough. "Pretty please?" I say through gritted teeth.

"Fine, but only because you begged." She grins and I bite my tongue before I say something stupid.

She's just trying to be cute, Maddox. She's purposely trying to get under your skin. Don't let her win.

It's a good thing she is cute. I shuffle to the table, refusing to put clothes on because if I can't mess with Friday since she holds too many cards right now, I'll mess with Callan.

"Tell Alec about that, and I'll chop off your nuts. Both of you." I point to them as I speak, and Lenny holds his hands up in surrender and Callan ignores me, continuing to eat his heaping pile of pancakes.

They're perfectly round, thick and fluffy. Just the way I like them. My mouth is watering as I watch him slice into the stack with a knife.

"Tell me what?" Alec asks. "Why the fuck are you naked?" We all turn to look at Alec, who is standing just inside the kitchen in nothing but pajama pants. No shirt. Alec isn't wearing a shirt. That is not normal. Really unlike him. He never walks around without his shirt on, not after what happened. Not even around us. His scars aren't as visible as they used to be, they're all mostly healed and have faded over the years, but they *can* still be seen if you look close enough. Fuck, I can't believe he's doing this in front of Friday. Especially after the way he's been since we met her.

I narrow my eyes and look back to Lenny and Callan, then over to Friday. I woke up in another dimension. There's no other explanation for his behavior, or the fact we have a woman in the kitchen cooking for us without bitching about it.

"Would you like some pancakes?" Friday asks, her golden gaze on him as she places a plateful in front of me.

"Sure." He pulls out the only remaining seat at the table and sits. I stare at him and blink. I wait for him to pull out his phone, but he doesn't. He just rests his elbows on the table, folding his hands to lean his chin on them. What the fuck is happening here?

"Are you feeling okay?" I ask him, tilting my head to the side. Something is very wrong here. He's being too nice, too fucking normal.

"I'm fine." He looks at me like I'm the crazy one, like me being naked is the wildest shit to happen ever. Because him coming out here, acting like part of us, talking to Friday and being nice about it, not wearing a fucking shirt, isn't the weirdest fucking shit ever.

"Are there more?" Lenny calls across the kitchen.

"She hasn't even eaten yet!" Callan snaps.

"Did I wake up in another reality or something?" I look around at all the guys, taking a second or two to really look at them and see if anything is off. I could be dreaming. Maybe I'm still sleeping, and this just feels real? I don't usually remember any of my dreams, and they've never been as vivid as this, but it's possible.

This feels too much like the old us. All of us here, around a table, eating, and without arguing.

It's weird as fuck.

I don't like it.

Something is really fucking wrong here.

"I'm making more... relax, guys." Friday says with a giggle.

Lenny gets up and goes into the living room to get the small wooden chair that pairs with the desk. He brings it back to the table and places it between him and I. It doesn't take long for Friday to walk over to us, balancing three plates in her hands. I give her a questioning look.

"What? I've waitressed once... or twice." The large platter gets put down in the center of the table, one plate goes to Alec, and the other to herself. She sits down, looking around at each of us with a satisfied smile on her face before she picks up her knife and scoops some butter to spread on her top pancake. She uses a small amount of syrup and then starts to eat.

When we are all finished eating, Callan speaks up—again, which really throws me for a loop. "Friday," he says calmly, folding his arms in front of him on the table. "Would you mind if I spoke to the guys privately?" Her eyes widen and she blinks, the look on her face not giving much away. She doesn't look offended, but maybe shocked?

"Of course not. I need to go through my stuff, anyway." She stands up and reaches for the dirty plates, but Lenny puts a hand up to stop her.

"We'll take care of it. It's only fair since you cooked," he says.

She nods once, then leaves the table. Just before she reaches the hallway, she stops and turns toward us. "If you guys want me to leave, could you give me at least a day? I have nowhere—"

"I assure you, it's not like that," Callan says quickly.

I sit back and cross my arms over my chest. What the fuck is happening here? Did I miss something? Was I sleeping so long they had a secret meeting or something? When did Callan grow a pair?

Friday gives us a small, sad smile, then hurries to her room, the door shutting softly behind her.

"Am I dreaming?" I ask as I turn back toward the guys. I'm met with confused stares. "You all are acting weird as fuck and it's starting to freak me out. Lenny is being quiet, Callan is talking, *willingly*... and to a *girl,* and Alec is fucking socializing with his *shirt off.* Have you guys lost your minds?"

Everyone looks around the table as if they hadn't noticed any of this.

Lenny reaches for another pancake, completely ignoring what I'd said, and drops it onto his plate and then says, "Before you start talking about whatever it is you need to say, it's Monday. You and Alec need to decide who is going to let Maddox feed. He won't let me do it."

So, we're just ignoring it all then. Okay, fine.

"I'll do it," they both say in unison. I slap my hand on the table.

"Someone better tell me what is going on right now."

Lenny's eyes widen, and he mouths a *wow.* Before cutting into his pancake and shoving a quarter of it into his mouth. "Are you guys still drunk? Did you take something?"

Again, I'm ignored, just looked at like I've lost my damn mind. Maybe I have.

"I will do it. Alec can do it next week."

"Works for me," Alec says, taking another pancake for himself.

I shake my head and lean back in my chair. I'm not going to get an answer here, so I may as well just let it go.

"We need to figure out a plan," Callan says. "Maddox and Lenny have made it clear what their thoughts on Friday are, and I can now confidently say I am on board as well." He's quiet for a moment, readjusts his glasses, and then continues talking.

"Alec, a lot rides on you, but before you say anything, just know that—"

"I'm in."

"You're in? Just like that?" I snap, my voice goes up a pitch. I am completely and utterly fucking shocked at what I am hearing. Alec is going to agree, just like that?

"Yeah, whatever," Alec grunts, shoving a bite of pancake into his mouth.

"Okay, that was simpler than I expected." Callan looks toward me, then says, "So, since we are all on board, now what? What is the plan?"

"Are you guys sure you're all feeling okay?" I ask again. "Do you have a fever? Headache?" I look at each of them, but none of them respond. They must be possessed. Robots? Fucking aliens? I stand up to walk over to the coffee pot, scratching my head as I go. I can't make sense of this. Nothing makes sense. Could it be the blood? Do I need more? Has finding her messed with *my* head?

"Maddox? The plan?" Callan's voice pulls me out of my thoughts.

I look down at the full pot of coffee.

"Has anyone had coffee yet?" I ask over my shoulder. They all shake their heads. Maybe that's it. No one is thinking clearly. We need coffee. Lots of fucking coffee. I grab the pot and four mugs and go back to the table. Callan heads to the fridge and pulls out a dish of half & half cups and some packets of sugar from one of the cabinets. I fill the mugs with coffee, and Alec snatches his up right away and starts to sip from it. I watch him carefully, half expecting him to tear his face off and show the alien that's taken control of him.

"I, uh..." I start as I sit down. "I haven't figured that out yet. What do you guys think?" The moment the words come out of my mouth, I can't believe I said them. I just asked their opinion on something. I don't bother mentioning it, don't bother pointing it out. For some reason, they don't see anything wrong with what's going on, so clearly, it's just me. Maybe, just fucking maybe, this is because of Friday. Because she is our missing mate, and we're together, and everything is falling into place. Just the way the prophet said it would. That explanation is something I can get on board with, so it's what I choose to tell myself.

I pour two of the half & half cups into my mug, watching the darkened liquid swirl to a lighter shade of brown as I mix it with the spoon, for some reason finding it mesmerizing. I blink a few times and shake my head. I need to get it together.

Callan pours a small amount of milk into his coffee, then adds his sugar as he continues on. "I think we need to tell her and then deal with what comes at us. We aren't going to know what she knows if we don't bring it up first. We can't expect her to tell us something like that."

"I can do it," Lenny offers, raising his hand while using the other to shove half a pancake into his mouth.

"That is probably the best idea. You guys seem to have hit it off well. Maddox?" Callan's green eyes meet mine, and there is something there. Something new that I've never seen before. Confidence? Hope? Determination? I don't have a fucking clue.

"Fine by me. As soon as possible." I look at Lenny, and he nods. "Reconvene next week, then?" If you can't beat 'em, join 'em, right? *Just go with it, Maddox. Go with it.*

They all nod their heads, but Alec's gaze lingers on me a moment too long and I raise a brow in question. "Can you put on some fucking clothes now?"

All I do is grin.

Chapter Twenty-Six

FRIDAY

The entire time I'm sorting my clothes, the butterflies in my stomach are going insane, and not for a good reason. I would hate it if they were trying to get rid of me. I know I don't have a place here with them, I have no right to be included in anything they do, but I've grown to like these guys. It's not just about having nowhere to go. That definitely sucks, but it's not what I'm struggling with. I like it here; I like being with them. Especially after this morning. Making them breakfast, all of us sitting there and eating together? It was so nice. It felt good. I've never felt anything like that before.

I knew this was going to happen, though, didn't I? I've been telling myself I needed to figure something out. I can't rely on anyone but myself. I can't expect these guys to just take me in. I know that now and I knew it when I first got into their car. So why am I so shocked by this?

I finish sorting through the clothes that are all over the floor, then I start to fold them all. I get to my feet and stare down at the piles of clothing, wondering what I should do with them. Should I put them away or put them back in the bags? Maybe I should buy a suitcase or a backpack like I'd planned back in Ellbrooke, this way it'll be easier to carry what I need. If these guys want me gone, I need to figure out the best way to bring all my stuff with me. Yes, Callan said he didn't want me to leave, but he could have just been being nice so I wouldn't freak out. Maybe they've left? Maybe they wanted to keep me occupied while they gathered their things and left without me. That would be awful.

A soft knock sounds at the door, I look over to it just as it opens and in steps Lenny.

"Hey, can we talk?"

"Ready to tell me to go?"

"No, silly. We want you to stay." He grins and shoves his hands into his pockets.

"Really?" I take a few steps toward him, but stop, unsure if he's messing with me.

"Uh, yeah. I don't plan on getting rid of you... uhm, ever."

My arms go around his neck and I leap into his arms, the amount of emotion running through me has me on the verge of tears. He hugs me around the waist and spins us, pressing a kiss to my neck. When he stops, I'm giggling and I pull back to look at him, taking his face between my hands.

"Are you sure?" I whisper.

"Super sure." He leans forward and kisses me, a firm peck against my lips. I hug him again, and then he puts me down. I turn toward all my clothes, happy that I'll be able to put them away now.

"Can we go by a store? I want to pick up a suitcase, or a backpack. Something better than these trash bags." I kick one with my foot.

"Anything you want," he tells me.

"I'm going to change. Meet you in five?"

He nods, places a kiss on my forehead, and walks out of the room. I make quick work of grabbing clothes and getting dressed. I use the tall mirror in the corner of the room to fix my semi-crazy hair. I run my fingers through it, getting out all the knots and then throw the top half into a messy bun, allowing the rest to stay around my shoulders.

Lenny is waiting for me on the couch in the living room with the other guys when I get out there. They're all together, watching a movie. Even Alec is there, focusing on the TV, his phone nowhere in sight. I didn't miss the fact he ate with us this morning and wasn't distracted by his phone.

"Ready?" Lenny asks when I reach the couch.

I nod my head eagerly. He stands and takes my hand, interlocking our fingers and then we head downstairs. It's gorgeous outside, the sun high and sky clear. For once, it doesn't look like it's going to rain. Lenny waves down a cab and we get in. He lets the driver know where we want to go and then we're on our way.

"Why'd we take a taxi instead of driving?" I ask as I watch the buildings we pass. There are so many things I'd love to check out, so many different restaurants, bookstores, music stores, and clothing shops. Would the guys be interested in doing that while we're here? I guess I'll have to ask.

He shrugs. "I thought it would be more of an adventure ."

He's so adorable.

I smile at him and nod. It was a good choice.

When we pull up in front of the store the taxi driver asks if we would like him to wait, but Lenny tells him no. I figured we would be quick, but Lenny said he wants us to take our time and look around. He wants to enjoy time with just us, which sends the little butterflies in my stomach into a frenzy, this time in the best possible way. He wants to be alone with me. Maybe there is a chance for something more between us? But what about him and Maddox? How would that work? God, all I can imagine is Lenny getting jealous down the line over knowing I fucked his best friend. Or rather, his best friend fucked me. And what if Maddox has feelings for me? I don't want to get in between them.

Okay, Friday, calm down. No one said anything about relationships. We're just having fun, nothing more.

We have too much fun while shopping. It's all laughing and joking, and pure fun. We found best friend t-shirts that we just had to buy. They each have a cartoon drawing on them, his is bacon and mine an egg. When side by side, they look like they're running toward each other. It's adorable.

I also find a keychain that I just have to buy for Maddox. I can't wait to give it to him. Aside from them, I get a decent-sized suitcase that should hold everything I'll need, while I can keep the other stuff stored in other trash bags. I was thinking of getting enough suitcases for everything, but after seeing how expensive they are and realized I would never use them again after this, I felt it wasn't a smart purchase.

We catch another cab back to the hotel, but hit a bit of traffic on the way, which is when I suddenly remember Lenny asked if we could talk earlier.

"What did you want to talk to me about before? I got so excited about staying with you guys that I forgot until just now."

"It can wait 'til we get back." He smiles and takes my hand.

The rest of the ride back is silent, we both keep our eyes glued out the window, watching the people, cars, and buildings we drive by. Lenny doesn't let go of my hand for even a second.

We get out of the taxi, and Lenny grabs the suitcase then tries to take the bag too, but I don't allow it. He's such a gentleman, but I want him to know I can take care of myself. I don't want him or any of them to think I'm helpless because I'm not.

We walk into the suite, and the kitchen and living room are empty. Lenny leaves the suitcase in my room and then runs to the bathroom. I dig into the bag and pull out the keychain I got for Maddox, laughing to myself as I head to his room.

"You make me wish I had more middle fingers." I read it to myself as I go and can't help but keep laughing. I find Alec's door closed, which isn't a shock, but Maddox's is partly open, so I knock quickly and then step in.

A loud gasp escapes my throat as both hands fly up to my mouth, causing me to drop the keychain to the ground. What I see renders me speechless, but a million thoughts run through my head. I have no idea how to react to what is going on in front of me, so I freeze. It doesn't last long though, because terror courses through me and I turn and run. I run all the way down the hall and out the door.

"What the fuck, Maddox?!" I hear Lenny shout before the room door closes fully.

I jab the button for the elevator too many times, knowing it won't make it come any quicker, but my anxiety and fear won't allow me to keep still. I keep looking back to the room, terrified one of the guys is going to come out here and follow me. The elevator door opens, and I dash inside, turning swiftly and stabbing madly at the button to close the door. "Come on! Come on!" I miss the button to close the door, and instead hit the button for the fourth floor. Either way, as long as the door closes and the elevator moves, I'm fine. Okay, definitely not fine but... anything is better than here.

When the doors finally close, I take a step back and realize how badly my body is trembling. I hear Lenny calling my name, even as the elevator descends.

"Please, please, please..." I beg under my breath, though I have no idea what I'm begging for. For him to leave me alone? For him to chase me and tell me I didn't see what I think I saw?

Everything around me starts to move in slow motion. I'm dizzy and feel as if I'm going to pass out. My heart, though? It's pounding in my chest, beating so hard I swear it's going to explode.

My shaky hands run down my face, then through my hair. I take a few long and deep breaths, trying to calm the fuck down. The elevator stops on floor six. I hold my breath as the door opens, worried it's one of *them*. When I see a woman and a child standing there, I release the breath quietly, trying to keep my shit together. They step onto the elevator and the woman checks the pad, noting the ground floor button is lit up. Then she and her child move to the opposite corner, and they don't say a word.

When the elevator stops on the fourth floor, no one says a thing, but when we reach the bottom, I rush through the main lobby and out the doors. I come to a stop right at the curb, looking both ways and trying to decide what to do.

I have no idea what to do. I have no idea where to go.

What did I get myself into? I knew this whole thing was too good to be true.

Did I really see what I think I saw? Is that possible? Why... why was that happening? It's impossible. It has to be impossible. Monsters aren't real. They aren't.

But Maddox was—his mouth was—fuck!

Fuck, fuck, fuck! What the fuck! I run my hands through my hair as I whirl around and walk the opposite direction of where we went last night, the thought of what I saw replaying over and over in my head. I pick it apart, trying to figure out if there was a way I didn't see what I saw. But I did... I know what I saw. I know what was happening.

Maddox was *drinking* Callan's blood. Like a... vampire. A vampire? *A fucking vampire.* His mouth was on Callan's wrist, blood outlining his lips and smeared on Callan's arm. Callan, who didn't look even the slightest bit disturbed by what was happening.

What the fuck is going on here?!

My feet move faster, needing to get as far away from this place as possible.

For the love of all things holy, Friday, how on Earth did you end up here?

Did they take me so they can eat me? Drink me? My god, when I joked about them killing me it was a joke! I didn't think they were serious!

And why were they waiting? Were they trying to fatten me up or something? Does that make a difference? I have no fucking idea. Not one fucking clue.

Wow.

Just *wow.*

I walk for what feels like an hour before I stop for a break. There's a bench by the curb, and I sit for a minute, just needing to relax. It's when I realize I have nothing with me but my phone. I left everything else there. *Everything*. My entire life is in that room. Every single belonging I have, and my purse! My purse with my wallet, ID, and money! How will I do anything without that stuff?

Fuck!

I should have waited to go into Maddox's room, but his door was open! It was fucking open!

"Maybe you're crazy, Friday." I say the words out loud, but I don't think I believe them. I know what I saw. Maddox's mouth...

The blood...

The moaning! Oh my god, Maddox was moaning. He-he was enjoying it!

I push myself up onto trembling knees and start moving again.

I walk down the busy street as quickly as I can, the sun shining brightly above me, with nowhere to go. It'll be dark soon, what then?

I pass dozens of people who have no idea what I've just witnessed. They have no idea what the hell I am struggling with. They're too busy battling their own demons or living in perfect harmony with their perfect fucking lives. Yet here I am. My world is crumbling around me. I have nothing but the clothes on my back, a cell phone in my pocket, and a brain full of fucked up memories.

I walk and walk and walk. I check my phone.

Nothing. I have no one to call, no one to call me.

I have nothing.

I stop when I find a park, deciding to walk through it. I come to a large open field and lower myself to the ground below a large oak tree. I try to even my breathing... deep breaths in, slow breaths out. The more relaxed I become, the more emotion washes over me. A lump forms in my throat as my chest tightens. I fight tears, knowing that crying isn't going to do a damn thing, but I can't help it. They fall, and it seems they only fall harder as I wipe them away.

After some time, they stop and I stare out into the field as the sun starts to set across from me, lowering behind the trees. There are a few people still in the field. Some passing a football back and forth, there's a guy playing fetch with a dog, and an older man just walking.

What am I going to do? I knew being with these guys was only temporary, but I still had about two weeks left! I can't stay with them now. I can't stay here at the park either. I have to at least go back to get my things. How am I going to do that? Now that I know their secret, they could kill me faster! They could be waiting for my return so they can tie me up and murder me!

What if I call the cops? They could escort me there, right? What the hell would I tell them though? If I told them the truth, certainly they'd think I was crazy. They'd end up throwing me in a loony bin. That is a place to stay though... I'd have food and shelter.

No, Friday, that's just ridiculous!

If I had a room key, I could sneak into the room. If I had any of the guys' numbers, I could demand they leave it downstairs. There are too many ifs and not enough solid ideas. It isn't going to help me now. I need a plan, a real plan.

Think, Friday. Think!

God, my chest aches. It hurts and feels so damn empty. I feel like I've just lost a piece of me, and I have no idea why. Yes, I've grown to like them, but how am I more upset over leaving them than I was over my boyfriend of four years? Tears well in my eyes again.

This truly can't be happening.

The weight of everything pulls me down, and I feel my body giving up. I rest my head back against the tree and close my eyes for just a few moments, needing to pull myself together again.

When I open them, it's almost completely dark. The sun is gone, but the light of the sunset can still be seen above the trees, the beautiful pinks and purples illuminating the sky enough that I can still see.

I hug my knees to my chest, rocking myself back and forth as I try to calm my racing thoughts. Maybe once I calm down, I'll be able to think straight. Maybe I should walk more, busy my mind with something else so I can think clearly. I don't have much time left here, so I need to hurry the hell up. I need to get over this, and quickly. It'll be completely dark soon, and I have no idea what kind of place this is. Is it dangerous? More dangerous than back at the hotel room?

Fucking hell, do I know anything?

I've never felt more helpless than I do right now, and that only angers me.

I'll give myself five more minutes, and then I need to go. I focus on breathing, on listening to the wind, the birds, the faint sounds of the cars in the road. As the seconds pass, I feel myself start to relax. I feel the calm washing over me, feel my body soothing itself.

Good, I can handle this, I tell myself. I just needed a few minutes to get myself together. Couple more minutes, then I'm leaving.

My breathing is slow and even as I take in the fresh air. My lungs feel good, my body feels good.

My body is overtaken by this warm, tingling sensation. The weight that was holding me down is gone, and I can breathe. My chest isn't tight, the lump in my throat is gone, and I'm no longer trembling.

I'm fine. I'm good. I got this.

I smile to myself, and then open my eyes. I'm met with something so unexpected, that all I can do is stare.

Lenny stands before me, just a few feet away. His hands are in his pockets and there's a frown on his face.

How the hell did he find me?

I don't freak out like I thought I would. I don't panic and feel like he's here to kill me. I'm calm and how fucked up is it that I feel safe?

"Friday, I need to tell you something."

I stare into his blue eyes that are so bright I swear it's the only reason I can see them in the light of the setting sun. My brain is telling me to run. This is the exact thing I was running from;

this is who I was trying to get away from. Yet, my body feels so at peace and I'm itching to reach out and touch him. I want him to wrap me in his arms and hold me tight, tell me that everything will be okay. Because for some reason, staring at him like this, I just know that it will be.

To find out if Friday goes back to the guys, grab the next book!
https://books2read.com/TRTT-Finding-Callan

Join my Mailing List!
Not only will you get four free stories, but you'll get updates on my books, adorable puppy photos, a hilarious meme, and book deals!

Author Notes

This series is my baby and these guys are some of my favorites! This was the first RH series I wrote so it has a special place in my heart, and I thank you all a million times for keeping this series alive.

Thank you for your support ♥

Follow me on your favorite platform...

click here!